Deadly secrets

Jay .H. Dee

This is a work of fiction. The characters, incidents, and dialogues are products of the author's imagination and are not to be construed as real. Any resemblance to actual events or persons, living or dead, is entirely coincidental.

Scriptures were taken from the King James Version of the Bible. Public Domain.

Cover Photos by Francesco Cura on DepositPhotos.com, and Jay .H. Dee.
Cover design by Jay .H. Dee, Victoria, Australia.

Deadly Secrets

ISBN 978-0-9942436-3-8

Dedicated to my mum.
Your love and support
mean more to me
than words can ever say.
I love you, Mumsy!

Acknowledgments

I just want to say a quick thanks to my husband, my family, my friends, and a special thanks to Lenore. You have read my books and been a constant source of encouragement.

It's supporters like all of you that keep me pushing to publish my books. Otherwise they would just sit unread on my computer wasting space. Thanks for sharing my dream.

Thanks to Jesus for giving me the courage to finally do something with what You have given me. I love you!

Prologue

The edgy computer technician hurriedly download-ed the last file. It was only a matter of seconds before the hacker tracing his signal would find him. Although Hayden had created a complex pathway, where his signal bounced around the world, the mastermind hunting him would be closing in fast. Much too fast! Who was this guy?

The downloading bar on his laptop screen edged from ninety-two percent to ninety-five, ninety-six, ninety-seven. It paused as though taunting him. Nine-ty-eight, ninety-nine. He held his breath and glanced at the timer on his watch. He had calculated the win-dow of opportunity his diversion would provide. Two minutes maximum. It was now ticking down from five seconds.

The green bar reached one-hundred percent and with a fearful flick, he hit the wireless switch on his laptop, effectively disconnecting his computer from the internet. He glanced at his watch in time to see the last second change to a zero.

He leaned back in his chair and ran his hands

through his hair, realising how frighteningly close he had come to discovery. Too close. He backed up the last lot of files he had copied onto a portable external hard drive. He could not afford to lose them.

His mind screeched to a halt. What if something happened to him? It wasn't altogether unlikely due to the nature of what he had discovered, or the fact that someone had figured out he had hacked into their system and they were trying to trace his location.

What if the hacker had actually been successful in getting past Hayden's diversion? A split second was a miniscule basket in which to place all of one's eggs.

He decided to separate the backup hard drive from his laptop just to be on the safe side. But where could he safely stash it and who could he trust?

Rylie.

In nervous, hasty movements he stowed the collation of his investigations in his friend's laptop case sitting by the filing cabinet. Rylie was undergoing a degree to become a computer technician and enjoyed what he called 'geek talk' with the Sydney University lab tech. The twenty-year-old would be back from the library any minute now.

Should Hayden tell him about the hard drive that was now in the young man's laptop case? No. Knowledge was dangerous.

Deadly Secrets

He zipped Rylie's case shut and quickly packed up his own gear. He wasn't due to knock off work for a few hours, yet he had to get his findings to the authorities before it was too late.

1

The two men came to a stop on the walking track that ran along the South Head of Port Jackson, Sydney. Kade wandered to the railing and with hands on his hips, surveyed the ocean stretching out before him. A fresh sea breeze tussled his sun-bleached hair, causing short riotous curls to dance around his tanned face. Warm brown eyes crinkled at the corners as he smiled with delight and drew in a lungful of salty air.

His gaze dropped to the ocean lapping at a rocky shelf at the base of the twenty-metre cliff they were on. The aquamarine water at the bottom deepened into rich cobalt blue as it stretched toward the horizon.

Lachlan Mackie was bent over double nearby with his hands on his knees breathing hard. Kade glanced at his friend and grinned.

"Mate, you sound like an old steam engine chugging up a hill!"

Lachlan glanced up from the footpath at his feet long enough to send him a withering glare. Kade only chuckled.

"Come on, we weren't jogging that fast," he cajoled, his brown eyes sparkling with mischief.

"Fast ... enough ... considering you ... woke me up ... before dawn ... and I haven't even ... had ... my first cup ... of coffee ... for the day," he panted and straightened to full height, quite a few inches shorter than Kade's six foot one stature.

Where Kade had sandy coloured hair and a muscular physique, Lachlan had short, straight dark hair and a wiry build. Their personalities were as far apart as light was from darkness and yet that did not seem to make a difference to their friendship.

"Well if you spent less time in front of a computer screen and more time in the outdoors with me, you'd be a whole lot fitter."

Lachlan's breathing slowly evened out. "We go surfing every weekend."

"Yeah, but surfing's not running." He grinned and gave his friend a hearty clap on his back.

Lachlan quickly caught his balance after the friendly blow and sidled to the railing. "What was that story again? You know, the one you told me the last time you dragged me out here at dawn."

Kade leaned his elbows upon the railing and glanced sideways at his friend. "The Dunbar shipwreck?"

"Yeah, I think that's the one." Lachlan rested his forearms on the railing as well and let his gaze drop to the boulders on the shelf at the base of the cliff.

It sure was a long way down. Kade's eyes lit with their usual animated gleam as he began to expound the well-known Sydney Harbour tale.

"It happened around midnight during a stormy gale close to where we are now on the South Head. It was August 20th, 1857 as the Dunbar arrived after a long voyage from England."

Lachlan smiled in amusement at his housemate's book-like narrative and intense tone.

"The captain was aiming for the entrance to Port Jackson, only in the storm he misjudged the ship's position and wrecked on the South Head. One-hundred and twenty-one people on board perished, all but one. Twenty-year-old crewmember James Johnson was washed onto a rock ledge. There he was rescued and ironically later became a lighthouse keeper in Newcastle, saving the sole survivor of another shipwreck, the SS Cawarra.

"Now, the part of the story that I like the best was written in a book I found in the library. It tells of the Macquarie light keeper and his wife the night the Dunbar sank." Kade's tone was laced with intrigue.

Lachlan seemed to lose concentration as he squinted to see something in the shadows of an overhang above the rock shelf to their left.

"The light keeper's wife awoke with a terrible nightmare that a ship had just wrecked and that a man was trapped on a rock shelf and needed help. Her hubby told her it was just a dream and she should go back to sleep. But she awoke again with the same nightmare."

Lachlan strode to the end of the walkway, several metres to his right to get a better view.

"Where are you going? I'm telling you a story." Kade felt slightly disappointed upon noticing he had lost his audience.

"There's someone down there on the rock shelf." Lachlan's eyes had widened with realisation and a measure of curiosity.

Kade's look was infinitely patient. "That's what I'm trying to tell you. The light keeper's wife kept dreaming someone was trapped down there and-"

"No, Kade, someone is actually down there." Lachlan pointed.

Kade frowned in puzzlement and trotted to his side for a better vantage point. His keen eyes swept the boulders on the shelf and rested upon a form wearing what appeared to be a purple t-shirt and black shorts. The figure was sprawled beneath a slight overhang at the base of the cliff. The rising tide was only a metre or so away from the mystery person's bare feet.

"Do you suppose they're dead?"

"Whoever it is, they're not moving." Kade swung a long leg over the railing and then the other.

Lachlan looked horrified. "What do you think you're doing?"

"What does it look like? I'm going down to check it out." Kade was undaunted by the ragged cliff he was about to descend.

"Are you insane? This isn't rock climbing at the gym. This is a cliff and you have no harness or ropes! If you fall you'll either land on the rocks and break every bone in your body. Or you'll land in the water and the waves will wash you into the rocks and then you'll break every bone in your body."

Kade snorted in amusement at his friend's pessimism as he found his first foothold. "I won't fall."

"Granted, you've got more lives than a cat. But even if you don't fall, how do you expect to get back up?"

"I don't. You're going to call triple zero and get emergency services out here. Whoever that is down there, they're in bad shape. Dead or alive, they've got to be picked up by the police."

Lachlan shook his head. His expression begged the question, how could Kade be so matter-of-fact? Kade admitted to himself that he was probably going to the aid of a suicide jumper or a washed up fisherman. Either way, he understood his friend's perspective. Lachlan obviously thought it wasn't worth risking his life over a dead body.

"We should just wait for emergency services to get here. Don't be an idiot!" He shouted the last words as Kade's head disappeared below the ledge. He growled with frustration when he was completely ignored.

Kade smiled to himself as he descended. He could hear Lachlan grumbling as he dug his cell phone from his pocket.

"I'm warning you for the last time, tell me what you know!" The demand was punctuated by a sharp blow to the twenty-year-old's left cheek.

Rylie Hunter cringed and then flexed his hurting jaw. Something warm trickled from his split lip down his chin. He strained against the ropes binding his hands to a chair in what appeared to be a dungeon.

But he knew better. This was the twenty-first century in Sydney, Australia. Places like this did not exist anymore. Yet here he was in a room that was dank and obscure. The air smelled musty, only with a hint of salty ocean. It was silent and would be pitch black were it not for the torchlight shining directly in his eyes. Where was he and who was this man holding him hostage?

Rylie's confused and terrified mind returned to a similar ordeal only four years ago. He had been kidnapped and drugged by order of the crooked ex-foreign minister of Australia, as a threat to his father's executive to continue his cooperation smuggling drugs through Ezekiel Hunter's shipping company. Rylie's mind reeled in shock. This could not be happening again!

"I told you I don't know," he answered with a swollen lip from an earlier blow he had received.

"You're lying. My sources say you're good friends with Hayden Brooker and spend time with him every day you're at university. He said he gave you something."

Rylie mentally scrambled to think of what he could be referring to. And how on earth did he know Hayden Brooker? Who were his apparent sources?

"I don't know what you're talking about. Sure I hang out with Hayden, but he didn't give me anything." Fear spiralled through him. What was this about?

The sinister voice lowered to a dangerous tone. "He did give you something."

"How do you know Hayden and what is it you think

he gave me?"

The kidnapper's breath brushed Rylie's left ear as the man spoke only inches away from his bruised face. "He told me moments before I terminated his existence that it was an external hard drive. Now if you don't want to suffer the same fate as he did, then tell me where it is!"

Rylie flinched as the man's volume increased and his left ear sharply protested the loud verbal assault.

"He's dead?"

Horror overcame him and his heart twisted with grief. First his best friend and now Hayden. He had lost them both within the span of a day, one awful, nightmarish day. How could this be happening?

Tears burned behind his eyes and a lump rose within his throat to choke him. His stomach churned sickeningly, and unable to do anything about it, he was promptly ill.

His captor exclaimed in disgust and leapt out of the way. The torchlight averted so that it was no longer blinding him. However, Rylie had neither the desire nor inclination to study his surroundings. He no longer cared. He would die soon, just as his best friend and Hayden had, and he would never know why.

2

Kade's runners finally touched down on the rock shelf roughly twenty metres below the top of the concave shaped cliff line. He turned from the jagged face he had just descended in the direction of the body. He could see it from where he was standing, directly across the turquoise water covering the lower ledge that was being quickly swallowed by the rising tide.

He trotted around the shelf, his feet nearly slipping at one point on weed covering the surface like a carpet. His long legs ate up the distance in seconds and he climbed over the last few boulders onto the upper ledge, where he could now clearly see a body sprawled face down.

Now only a few metres away, he saw long brown hair and a slim, shapely form. His steps slowed and dread sank like a rock to the pit of his stomach. It was a woman. How had she ended up down here? Had she jumped? Had she fallen overboard at sea and washed ashore?

He knelt beside her. "God, please let her be alive?"

His fingers felt for a pulse in her slender neck and a shallow but steady rhythm met his touch. He glanced back up to where he knew Lachlan was watching from the top of the cliff.

"She's alive!"

His friend looked significantly small against the jagged rock face towering high above. Lachlan's tiny arm waved and his voice drifted down.

"Help's on the way!"

Kade waved in acknowledgement and turned his full attention to the unconscious woman beside him. He gave her right shoulder a squeeze. "Can you hear me?"

This received no response. Her left cheek was pressed against the rock and thick wet hair covered the half of her face that he could see. Acting against all good sense, he placed his hand on her left shoulder and rolled her over into his arms using his right.

A groan came from cold, blue lips and his heart leapt into his throat. That was better than no response at all. Then he saw it.

Blood. Lots of it.

An inch above her left ear was a nasty gash that had obviously bled profusely. However, much of it had dried and caked in her hair, suggesting the wound was several hours old. How long had she been down here? Her skin was chilled beneath his fingers.

Did she have hypothermia?

He used a tone people rarely argued with. "I know you can hear me. I need you to wake up."

Her eyes remained closed and her body motionless, except for the gentle rise and fall of her chest. He quickly removed his windcheater, and with a little manoeuvring, managed to pull it over her head. He paused.

What was that dark colouring on her upper arms? He frowned and carefully studied the nasty bruises on her biceps. They looked like large hand and finger marks. Not liking the conclusion his mind was coming to, he dropped the matter and quickly threaded her arms into the sleeves.

Then he drew her against his chest to provide warmth. He figured he should probably be checking for other injuries but reckoned in the end the cold and that nasty head injury were the greatest threats to her life right now.

"Come on." His gaze lifted to Lachlan and then searched the ocean before him. How would emergency services choose to get her out of here? By chopper, by boat, or by scaling the cliff? He figured boat was the best bet.

"Time for you to wake up."

He studied her youthful face. She could not be more than twenty. Had someone pushed her over the cliff? The bruising on her upper arms seemed to indicate some kind of struggle.

"Lord, only you know what really happened, and I thank You that she's alive. If it's okay with You, she really needs Your help."

He continued to pray as he waited for help to arrive. It finally showed up in the form of a police boat speeding around the South Head.

The darkness was so thick around Rylie he thought it would almost be possible to cut it with a knife. At first the silence had been oppressive, plagued by fear and pain. Now, hours since the abrupt departure of his captor, his mind had cleared through prayer. His heart had become peaceful. It caused him to think of Paul and Silas when they had experienced God's presence after being beaten and thrown into prison.

Having reached the end of his strength and ability, Rylie supposed he was in the perfect place for a miracle of his own. Besides, he had to survive, if only to find out what had become of his best friend.

"Heavenly Father, I really need Your help. Will you please get me out of here? I don't need an angel like Peter or an earthquake like Paul and Silas. Just something simple will do."

He waited for an answer for a full minute. He shifted and the chair creaked. The noise drew forth a memory. Just last year he had been sitting at the dinner table in a metal framed chair much like this one, with a glossed wooden seat. He had leaned back and the hollow frame had buckled and broken at the welds. His mother had been most put out.

Hope went on in Rylie's mind like a lamp in darkness. "That could work."

He twisted his hands against the ropes binding them to the cylindrical metal tubing. As he felt with his hands he smiled. Yes, there were welds at the joins between the frame to which his hands were tied, and the circle upon which the seat itself was attached. His feet were bound to the chair legs, but if he could use his weight, he might be able to tip it enough to put some serious stress upon the joins.

Rylie threw back his weight and the chair lifted off its front legs. It teetered dangerously and he let out a surprised yelp as it fell. His head and shoulders crashed into solid cement and then the back of the chair connected with the wall too. It scraped downward for an uncomfortable moment and then stopped its descent.

Rylie cringed and wished he could rub the knot developing quickly on the back of his head. His neck protested at the odd angle it was forced to endure.

The chair creaked ominously, hollow metal joints began to sag, and he wondered how much more of this awkward position he could tolerate.

"This was your idea, God, and it was a good one. I'm not complaining." His teeth clenched. "But do You suppose You could sort of speed up the process?"

The stressed welds let out a groan and so did the prisoner. Rylie pushed backward to apply more pressure. Suddenly there was a pop and the left side bent and snapped free. The chair slipped to the floor and Rylie landed with a thud and rolled onto his side, seat and all.

He pulled his left hand along with the rope, off the frame and brought his hand to his mouth. He cringed when rough rope met with his split lip. After much chewing and tugging, he managed to loosen the rope enough to slip his hand out.

Although it was awkward and difficult in pitch-black darkness, desperation and a sense of urgency spurred him onward. He loosened the ropes binding his feet to the chair legs one at a time. When his feet were free, he stood and picked up the chair. He jammed the back against the wall and the legs against the floor.

Using his weight, he leaned on it until the last weld between the seat and the frame weakened and buckled. He twisted it and applied more pressure. It came free. He slipped his hand over the broken end and quickly worked to loosen the rope still tied around his wrist.

Another two minutes of grappling with the knot using his free hand and his teeth proved successful. He slipped his fingers out and tossed the rope aside. His hands found the wall and he felt his way along for several metres until they came to rest upon solid steel. He pushed against it and it made a metallic clank. It had to be a door.

He felt his way across it, thinking to find the wall into which it was built. Instead he encountered cement running adjacent to the wall he had just followed. He wasn't in a room. It was a tunnel.

He followed the wall back the other way, running into another steel door. It did not budge either. His captor had obviously locked the doors from the outside.

Frustrated and somewhat dejected, he felt his way toward the other end. Halfway there he paused, noticing something he had overlooked in his initial desperation. A cool, salty draught whispered down from above. It smelled like the ocean. Could it be an air vent?

He fumbled in the darkness for the broken chair, eventually bumping into it with his right shin. He gritted his teeth to keep from growling and stood still until the pain abated. When the stinging sensation lessened to a dull ache, he picked up what was left of the seat and carried it back until he could feel the gentle salty breeze drifting down from above.

Rylie placed the chair with its four legs on the cement floor, frowning a little as it wobbled. Hmm, he had obviously managed to buckle the back two legs in his bid to break free. He mentally shoved his concern aside and climbed onto the seat, hoping it would hold his weight and that he would not lose balance.

He reached upward, and being naturally tall, his hands easily touched the ceiling. It too was rough and cold like cement. No wait. Was that metal his fingers brushed by?

The chair groaned and wobbled and Rylie carefully repositioned his weight by shifting his feet further apart. At the same time his fingers roamed the ceiling. Yes, there it was. His touch met with cold steel in the shape of what felt like a grid.

He pushed up and metal scraped upon cement, resistant but gradually giving way. Finally he held its full weight in his hands and pushed it up and aside. Dried leaves dropped downward like a fall of snowflakes. Dust accompanied the downpour, easily finding his face.

Rylie coughed and blinked. His eyes were stinging.

Moonlight now filtered down in a shaft, no longer blocked by leaves and undergrowth. He reached and grasped a hold of the outside edges of the vent. He swung his legs up, caught his heel upon the ground outside and then the other. With some wriggling and painful scrapes and bruises, he squeezed himself out of the hole.

He rubbed sore, watery eyes. Finally the world around him came into view and he was stunned to discover exactly where he was. A large patch of closely cropped grass lay just beyond the shrubbery in which he was standing. To his right the ocean stretched calm and quiet, sparkling in full moonlight and washing against the cliffs.

He could see the North Head of Port Jackson across the gap. Close by, the Hornby Lighthouse stood tall with red and white vertical stripes, glowing brightly in the night to safely guide ships into the harbour.

Rylie was amazed. He had been held captive in the underground tunnel that joined the gun emplacements on the South Head, a relic from 1854.

Knowing that his captor would likely return, he started down the walking track at a jog. Where should he go? He couldn't go home. His captor seemed to know everything about him. He would know where he lived.

Who could he call? His parents were on a tour

of Europe and would not return for another three weeks. The police? Yes! He cringed. He had left his cell phone in his laptop case and he now realised he had accidentally forgotten to take his laptop from beneath his seat on the ferry. He would have to find a pay phone or maybe even knock on someone's door and beg to use their telephone.

He remembered the moment he became embroiled in this mess and decided that first he would head to the cliffs on the ocean side of Watson's bay. It had to be at least twenty-four hours since it had happened and he doubted he would find her. Nevertheless he had to try.

3

"Her CAT and MRI scans gave no hint to haemor-rhaging, although the brain shows signs of trauma, such as swelling and bruising around the left parietal lobe. In short there is no telling what damage has been done until she wakes up," a male voice floated around the edges of the patient's consciousness.

It was joined by another. "So you're saying that although there seems to be no immediate threat, there could be some permanent damage?"

"There are no guarantees with head injuries, you know that. This coma could last hours, days or worst case scenario, months or even years."

"You're the neurologist, what do you recommend we do?"

"The usual for now. Keep an eye on her vital signs tonight. The drip will keep her hydrated and tomorrow we will put in a feeding tube if she has not woken up. I will stop by in the morning to see how things are progressing."

"Alright. I'll brief the nurses."

Footsteps receded and other unfamiliar sounds

penetrated the haze surrounding her brain. An intermittent buzz, male and female voices conversing in the distance, foot scuffs on linoleum, the sound of trolley wheels and curtains being drawn nearby.

Although unable to pinpoint the noises to a particular setting, they drew her from the dark abyss of unconsciousness.

The patient opened heavy eyelids. The room was dimly lit by light spilling in from an open doorway. Still she squinted against the brightness while her eyes adjusted. Her bleary vision focused upon a white ceiling and equally white walls. A soft olive coloured curtain to her left blocked her view of what she now presumed was another hospital bed.

She became acutely aware of a throbbing sensation above her left ear. She was in hospital and it made sense. With the way the whole left side of her head ached, she felt as though she had been walloped by a plank.

How had she ended up here and how had she injured herself? She wracked her brain for answers to questions that were beginning to pile high. Even more disconcerting was the blank slate that was her mind.

No memories. No past. No knowledge of self. Only a present circumstance she could not understand. Her confusion gave way to fear. Who was she and what had happened?

Rylie's thumb paused mid air above the buttons on the cordless telephone in his hand. The old lady who had kindly let him into her small cottage to use her telephone, was bustling about the kitchen just off the small living room.

Rylie was standing in the lounge by a small sofa, cordless phone in hand. To his right was a well-worn recliner. Tightly packed between the sofa and the recliner was a round table upon which rested a lead light glass lamp, a rosebud coaster and an empty coffee cup. The furniture faced a television in the corner that was switched on and loudly blaring the evening news into the room.

Beside it was a tall bookshelf cluttered with a variety of new and old tattered books, magazines and a myriad of dust collecting ornaments. On the wall adjacent to the television was a window looking out onto what he presumed was a garden. It was difficult to tell in the dark. On the opposite wall was the main entrance to the house, through which he had entered.

Rylie absently wondered if news of what had happened last night would be showing this evening. He shook his head and redirected his attention to the urgent call he needed to make.

"The body of a man in his mid twenties was discovered early this morning in the Sydney botanic gardens by a jogger," the anchorwoman informed.

Her report received Rylie's full attention and he disconnected the line he had just dialled. He listened in horror as the details of what was clearly a murder were elaborated on.

"Police found evidence at the scene that has led them to believe the crime may have been committed by a friend of the victim. The suspect, a twenty-year-old man by the name of Rylie Hunter, is currently at large and anyone having any information of his whereabouts is to contact Crime Stoppers immediately."

Rylie's face drained of colour as his picture flashed on the screen. He recognised it straight away. It was the photo that sat on the mantle above the fireplace in his parents' home. His kidnapper, the actual murderer had framed him! But how? What 'evidence' had been found?

He glanced at the cordless phone in his hand and then tossed it on the sofa as though burned. He could not call the authorities. They believed he had murdered Hayden. He had an alibi, but she was gone. Rylie had not found any trace of her at the cliffs.

There was no way she could have survived the fall, let alone the rocks and then the waves crashing upon them at the bottom. That knowledge alone left him feeling bereft.

Nevertheless, he had to clear his name before he could come forward about what had happened, or the killer would continue to roam free wreaking havoc with people's lives. The only way to clear his name and get justice for his friends' deaths was to find his laptop in its case.

He had to get to the bottom of why they had been targeted, and that seemed to revolve around the external hard drive the killer said Hayden had planted.

"Lachie, have you seen my wallet?" Kade shouted as he lifted a pile of clothing and some objects on his bedroom floor.

"Beats me," Lachlan's voice called back from the living room where he was no doubt sitting at his computer.

It was was set up on a desk at a large window overlooking the cove.

"You're lucky you don't get lost trying to find your way out of there every morning! Your room is a disaster zone."

"You're not helping! I'm gunna be late for church."

"So go without it." Lachlan sounded nonchalant. Kade understood why. They went through this ritual at least once a day. Yesterday it was his shoes that were missing and the day before it was his sunglasses. Now it was his wallet. Kade strode to the living room doorway.

"Big whoop." Lachlan checked his website to see how many hits it had received since yesterday.

With hands on his hips, Kade pondered a solution to his dilemma. "Maybe we should hire a cleaner?"

Lachlan snorted and smiled in amusement. "Don't bother. Just back burn it and start again."

Kade sent him a dry look. "Very funny."

Lachlan shrugged, his eyes glued continuously to the computer screen.

"Well, I'm going. I'll be back around lunchtime. Hey, do you wanna go surfing this afternoon?" Kade stuffed his feet into a pair of dress shoes that hadn't seen a lick of polish since the day they walked out of the store.

Lachlan glanced at his disorganised housemate. "Sure."

"Alright!" Kade grinned and brought his fist down in a gesture of victory. He exited the house and a second later the door opened and his head popped in again. He reached onto the side table beside the entrance and grabbed his sunglasses with a sheepish grin.

Lachlan chuckled. "Just as well your head's permanently attached, mate, or you'd forget that too." He returned his gaze to the computer in front of him.

Kade closed the door, already anticipating a great morning in church.

The curtain to the patient's left had been drawn back when the person sharing the room was removed earlier that morning. Now sunshine streamed from the window near the second bed.

She turned the wallet over in her hands and wondered how it had been overlooked. She had found it inside the windcheater stashed in the set of drawers beside her bed.

The neurologist had visited her not long after she had woken up and countless nurses had come and gone since then. The neurologist said it was retrograde amnesia. Giving the condition a name did not make her feel any better or gain the answers she needed. But this wallet might.

They had talked of more tests and had contacted the authorities to help search out her identity. An officer had been in that morning to take her prints and get a photograph. Nevertheless, they could not understand the horrible displacement she was experiencing or the desperation to own a sense of self. No, she would not wait for them or waste any more time on useless tests.

She opened the wallet and pulled out a driver's licence. She studied the photograph of a good-looking man with short curly blond hair above an address.

"How do I know you, Kade Haynes, and how did I end up with your wallet?" Curiosity demanded she find out. She supposed she should ask the police.

Desperation arose within her. No, she needed to contact this man personally and today! If he knew her, he would have the answers to her questions and hopefully be able to provide her with an identity. A name would lead to a past and a sense of belonging, maybe even a family.

She climbed out of bed and held onto the draws as the world spun around her. Gradually the dizziness receded to a manageable level and she removed the drip from her hand. She winced with discomfort as the needle came clear of her skin. She tossed it aside and stuck the tape and cotton wool back over the pinprick that was now bleeding.

Having freed herself of the annoying attachment, she pulled on the clothing stowed in the drawers. The t-shirt and shorts were dirty, but dry. The windcheater was relatively clean, somehow unscathed by whatever accident she had been involved in. There were no shoes, but at this point she did not care. She just wanted answers.

With the wallet stuffed into her pocket, she went to check out. There would no doubt be serious ob-jections, however she was determined that nothing would stand between her and the past she sought.

4

It had been an interminably long night and Rylie was exhausted. He had used his weekly public transportation ticket and caught a late ferry from Watson's Bay to Circular Quay, after hastily leaving the old lady's house.

It was Saturday night in Sydney which meant that the city was wide awake and teaming with life. He rested somewhat in the knowledge that if people were out dining and seeing the sights, then they had probably missed the evening news.

He had wondered how on earth he would retrieve his laptop. Where did lost property go? On the off chance that it had not yet been discovered, he waited a good hour for the exact ferry he had left it on to arrive at the dock.

Each of the eight inner harbour ferries, The Borrowdale, Alexander, Friendship, Fishburn, Sirius, Scarborough, Golden Grove, and Charlotte, were named after each of the original first fleet ships.

With a desperate plea heavenward begging God to still let it be there, Rylie boarded The Alexander and strode directly to the seat he had occupied on his trip to Watson's Bay. He reached under the seat where he had tucked it and let out a relieved breath and a grateful prayer. It was still there.

He quickly disembarked before the ferry could take off. Unfortunately he had nowhere to go, so he caught the first bus that came along and ended up in the suburbs. Not really knowing where he was headed and too exhausted to care, he wandered aimlessly.

Finally he found an old Anglican church in a backstreet with ancient headstones in the graveyard beside it. Huge gnarled trees shaded the quiet yard and he sank down against an enormous grave marker and fell asleep, laptop case clutched to his chest.

Sunday dawned bright and clear way before he was ready. He was starving, bruised and in sore need of a shower and more sleep. The first thing he decided to do was find an obscure cafe and get something to eat. Then he would fire up his computer and take a look at the external hard drive that was indeed tucked away in his laptop case.

She glanced again at the licence, positive she had the correct address, and strode through the open gate past a white picket fence. With one last look at the picture on the licence, she closed the wallet. She had the man's face memorised so it really wasn't necessary.

She knocked on the front door of a small house along the street backing onto a beautiful cove with squeaky white sand. The house was a light shade of blue with white trim around the window frames. It was relatively old in style, possibly early 1900's, and had a small dormer window peering down at her from what must be an attic. It was utterly charming.

Lining the front porch was a bed of roses in a variety of colours. The grass in the small front yard had been recently mown, although weeds popped up their noxious heads alongside the flowers in the garden, suggesting that whoever lived here was either extremely busy or simply did not care to tend it regularly.

She heard footsteps approaching on the other side and trained her eager attention on the door. The hinges groaned in protest as it creaked open. Standing in the entrance was a young man roughly in his early twenties, of medium height with straight black hair and a wiry build. His clear green eyes were framed by long dark lashes any woman would be jealous of.

This was not the man from the licence. His dark eyebrows shot up in surprise and he stared at her speechlessly.

She wasn't sure what to make of his response. "Hi. I was wondering if Kade Haynes lives here?"

He finally broke his stunned silence. "Yeah, but he's not in at the moment. Aren't you the girl we found yesterday morning?"

Uncertainty clouded her innocent expression. "I don't know. Am I?"

"That's what I asked you."

Doubts plagued her. "You don't know me."

His brows drew together in a suspicious frown. "What is this? I just said we only laid eyes on you yesterday. Look, if this is some kind of scam, you'd better try it on someone else. I'm not buying it."

She frowned in bewilderment. What was he talking about? "This isn't a scam. Never mind. Here." She handed him the wallet. "I found this in my pocket. I don't know how it got there."

Still looking puzzled and a little suspicious, he took it from her. Feeling dejected at hitting a dead end and a little frightened of the uncertain future, she turned and walked down the short stone footpath and through the gate.

Completely rattled and not knowing what to do or where to go, she headed for the beach. She needed some time to think and plan another strategy. This one had failed dismally.

Deadly Secrets

Kade walked in the front door around noon, kicked off his shoes and headed straight for his room. There he changed into a pair of white board shorts and a green t-shirt. He removed his socks and tossed them over his shoulder onto the floor as he exited his bedroom.

He headed to the kitchen to scrounge up something edible. On his way into the main living area, he cast a glance at his housemate. Lachlan was still sitting in the same place he had left him two hours ago, at his desk staring at the computer screen.

"Don't you ever get sick of sitting in front of that thing?" He was unable to comprehend the draw the machine had upon his friend. "You should get out more. You know, in the real world where normal people live and do everyday stuff."

"I will. We're going surfing this afternoon, remember?" Lachlan's tone held only a hint of irritation.

Kade stared into the nearly empty refrigerator. "I'll bet if computers were waterproof you'd take one along."

"Yeah, I'm just hanging out for the day."

A half smile tugged at the corner of Kade's mouth over Lachlan's dry quip. He closed the refrigerator and opened the pantry. Food was a little scarce in there as well. Thankfully there was a full loaf of bread and plenty of peanut butter. He placed both on the counter and was rummaging for a knife when Lachlan finally detached himself from his computer screen and wandered to the kitchen.

He sat on a barstool on the other side of the counter and watched Kade slather three slices of bread and clamp another three slices on top of those.

"You had a visitor while you were out."

Kade glanced up curiously from his sandwiches. Lachlan appeared to be puzzling over the encounter.

"Yeah? Who?"

"The chick you saved yesterday. She asked for you and I told her you were out. She brought back your wallet. The weird thing is, she thought I knew her."

He had Kade's full attention now. "Why would she think that?"

"Beats me. She's still sitting out there on the beach. Hasn't moved for about an hour."

Kade frowned in bewilderment. That was odd. Completely forgetting about his sandwiches, he strode to the window that overlooked the small azure cove.

A father and his son were swimming in the shallow waves and several people dotted the white sand sunbaking. Sitting far enough away from them all to gain a little privacy was a woman wearing a purple t-shirt and black shorts. Long brown hair flowed down her back and his windcheater was tied around her waist. Her knees were drawn to her chest and she sat motionless, staring out into the blue waters of the harbour.

She had not awakened at all yesterday morning, not even when the police picked them both up and took them into Watson's Bay, where they were met by an ambulance. He'd had the awful impression that she might very well die of that head wound. And yet there she sat on the beach outside his house, very much alive.

A sucker for injured animals and hurting souls, Kade felt compassion well up within him. He strode to the front door and straight out onto the footpath in bare feet.

"Where are you going?" Lachlan asked from the doorway.

"To see if she's alright," he threw over his shoulder. "Something you should have done earlier."

Lachlan rolled his eyes and closed the door.

"God, if You're there, and somehow I know You are, please help me?" She felt tears sting the back of her eyes. "What am I supposed to do?"

She stared out over the harbour, watching a white clipper speed past the cove fast on the heels of two others. This really was a beautiful place. It had a secluded feel about it. She liked that. It felt safe, something she had not experienced since awakening in the hospital.

Pure white sand squeaked under approaching bare feet. She expected the sound of footfalls to continue past her, as they had been doing for the past hour. But they did not. She sensed a large presence behind her and then he sat down to her right. She glanced in surprise at the stranger beside her and recognised sun-bleached fair-haired curls and warm brown eyes.

"You're Kade Haynes." Wonder lit her gaze and she dared to hope that the ease with which he joined her on the beach meant that he knew her.

"Yup. Lachie said you came to see me earlier."

He was open and straightforward. She liked that. Looking into those kind eyes, she knew her prayer had been answered. "I was hoping you might know who I am."

His brows flew upward, much like his housemate's had.

"I know that must sound strange. All I remember is waking up in hospital last night with a roaring head-ache and feeling terrified because I couldn't remember anything." She held his gaze and watched as he shifted his line of vision to the harbour. "I thought maybe you might be able to help me since I found your wallet in my pocket."

He was silent for several unnerving minutes. Should she say something? But what could she say? If he didn't believe her, she certainly wasn't going to try convincing him. On the other hand, if he knew her it would be plain to see she was not lying.

She had considered the dark haired man's reaction earlier. He had thought she was trying to pull a scam in order to get something from him and she could now understand why he would think that. Retrograde amnesia was farfetched. It was also a terrifying reality.

"And here I was all hopeful that a pretty girl sought me out 'cos she was interested. Turns out she was just being honest and returning my wallet." He threw his hands up in defeat. "Not that I'm ungrateful." His eyes gleamed mischievously. "I'll be needing it."

Her brows knit in a baffled frown and yet she could not help smiling at the same time. Being teased was the last reaction she had expected.

Her frown eased into a full blown smile at the relaxed expression on his face. It evidenced an easygoing nature. "Do you know how it ended up in my pocket?"

He smiled in amusement. "Sure I do. It's my pocket."

The frown returned. "This is your jumper?" Her hand dropped to the windcheater tied about her waist.

"When I found you on the rock ledge below the cliff, you were unconscious and freezing cold. I put my jumper on you. Hope it was clean."

Finally getting some answers, she ignored the cheeky sparkle in his eyes and shifted in the sand to face him directly. "Tell me what happened?"

Kade allowed the soberness apparently in his soul to show through his otherwise unruffled veneer. "I don't know. Lachie and I were jogging early yesterday morning and stopped at the lookout for a breather. He spotted you on the rocks below and called triple zero while I climbed down to where you were. I have no idea how you got there."

"And you really don't know who I am?" Keen disappointment crushed her hope.

"Not a clue." His gaze shifted to the left side of her face.

Her cheekbone was dark with bruising and the discoloration spread back into her hairline.

"Shouldn't you still be in hospital? Your head was pretty banged up and bloody yesterday morning."

She sighed and pulled her long legs to her chest,

resting her chin on her knees. "To be honest with you, I don't feel all that well, but I had to get some answers."

"Sorry I couldn't help." He studied her closely.

She had the impression he could see she was hurting and sensed her confusion. She looked into his open face and saw that he was genuine. It gave her comfort. "Thanks for what you did."

He smiled. "Anytime."

She observed him thoughtfully and finally spoke what was on her mind. "I'm glad I met you, Kade Haynes. Something tells me you're not the average run of the mill guy."

He chuckled and got to his feet. "Lachlan would disagree with you."

She smiled and rested her chin on her knees again. It had been nice conversing with someone who cared. Now what? Back to the hospital? She shuddered. Anywhere but there!

Kade stood beside her debating what to do. Would she be alright if he left? If she had a family, why hadn't they missed her and gone to the authorities who would have told them exactly where she was? Yet she was asking him the kind of questions kinfolk should be answering.

If he was her best bet, and only then because his wallet had been in the pocket of the windcheater he had loaned her, surely she had no one. Or at least not anyone who had noticed her disappearance.

"It was nothing. Thanks for your help." She offered a distracted, sad smile and returned her gaze to the water, ending the conversation and offering him an opportunity to leave guilt free.

'... whosoever has this world's goods, and sees his brother in need, and shuts up his heart from him, how does the love of God abide in him?'

The familiar Bible verse popped into Kade's thoughts unexpectedly and challenged him.

Okay God, I get the point. What do you want me to do?

Whosoever has this world's goods... The thought dangled in answer.

He crouched beside her, elbows on his knees. She turned to look at him questioningly.

"Don't s'pose you need a place to stay for awhile?"

She stared at him in silence for a full minute, confounded. Her questioning eyes were asking why he would offer hospitality to a complete stranger.

His hands came up defensively. "I don't want you to think I'm some kind of creep or anything. I just figured you might not have anywhere to go."

She smiled. "I know you're not a creep. You've got an honest face and I can see you're a caring person."

A chuffed grin lit his face. "You really think I'm all that?"

She could not resist a smile of amusement. He noticed her doting expression and quickly wiped the smile off his face.

"I mean, it's good you don't think I'm some kind of wacko," he tried a serious tone, which only made her smile broaden. He abruptly stood and scratched the back of his head in awkward silence.

She laughed heartily and released the tension inside her. Kade smiled sheepishly and nodded in the direction of his house.

"Come on."

She smiled and got to her feet. Her world must have tilted dangerously on its axis, for she stumbled. He reached out a hand and grasped her wrist.

"Steady as you go." He worried she might not be as well as she looked. He covered his concern with banter. "You should take it easy on the booze this time of day. A nice girl like you should know better."

She chuckled and straightened, blinking to clear her vision.

He dropped the pretence of humour. "Are you alright?"

"I will be. The doctor says I've got a nasty concussion. He said the symptoms should clear up soon. There's nothing for you to worry about."

"Yeah well, that's debatable." He took her other arm in his free hand, aware that if he wasn't holding her, she would undoubtedly fall.

"I'll be okay in a minute or so." She blinked several times in an attempt to dispel the dizziness and looked relieved when it subsided. "I think I can stay on my feet now, thank you."

He reluctantly let go. She was as white as a sheet and still looked a little unsteady. However, he let the matter drop and started up the beach for the footpath that led around to the front of his house. Thinking she needed a little light heartedness in her situation, and wanting to hear that bubbly laughter again, he put on a boyishly excited expression.

"I can't wait to see Lachie's face when I tell him I'm bringing home a pet." He rubbed his hands together.

She raised one eyebrow but was unsuccessful in trying to hide the amusement she felt. "So that's what I am now, your pet?"

He looked at her through large, disheartened eyes. "You don't want to be?"

"I'm not much good at playing fetch," she remarked dryly.

"Oh." He looked disappointed, then suddenly brightened. "Can you wash dishes?"

She could not resist the laughter bubbling inside her. It rang in the air like a jubilant bell and Kade smiled.

His brown eyes took on a warm sparkle. "Now that's what I like to hear."

"I've changed my mind. You are a bit of a nut."

Kade beamed and took it as though it was a compliment. "Yeah, Lachie thinks so too."

Uncertainty seemed to drop over her suddenly like a dark cloud. "What will he say when you tell him you offered for me to stay awhile?"

Kade grinned mischievously. "It's going to be great! I can't wait to see his reaction!"

She chuckled at the wicked pleasure he got from vexing his housemate.

5

Rylie took a sip of coffee and replaced the paper cup on the secluded corner table in Kentucky Fried Chicken. The restaurant was off the beaten path in Ashfield. He had been there since nine o'clock and it was just nearing lunchtime. Thankfully the place was still relatively empty.

He had his laptop plugged into a socket nearby and was sifting through the enormous amount of data and documents stored in Hayden's external hard drive. There were scanned copies of enrolment forms from Sydney University of three international students. Rylie recognised the name of one, Fahim Gabir. They were both undertaking the same computer technician course. He was a nice enough young man, although he tended to keep to himself most of the time.

There were other files as well, including lists of mobile phone records, low-resolution photographs, presumably taken using a cell phone camera. There were bank records, e-mails, private internet chat sessions obtained probably through spyware. He found encrypted files that would take some work to analyse, and a myriad of other documents that made no sense to him.

How were they all connected? Why had Hayden been collecting such an odd assortment, many of them from company and private records? Rylie did not want to even think about how his friend had acquired them.

A gentleman in his late sixties sat down on a bench against the wall nearby. He placed a tray laden with scrumptious smelling food on the table before him and slapped a newspaper beside it.

Rylie's attention went back to his computer screen. The newspaper snapped open and crackled. He glanced over momentarily and then spun back for a second surprised look. The gentleman had opened first to the sports section at the back. However, what captured Rylie's interest was a picture of himself staring at him from the front page. In dismay, he read the caption above it.

'Computer technician murdered when he threatened to reveal underground piracy racket.'

What on earth? Piracy racket?

He had never burned an illegal disc in his life, and refused to accept pirated goods on principle. Someone was working very hard to frame him. Steely determination hardened his resolve.

"You can bet I'm going to find out who."

The gentleman lowered the paper and looked at him curiously. "You talking to me?"

Rylie's glance slid nervously from the man's face to the picture on the front cover. "No, just talking to myself." He pasted on a friendly smile and quickly packed up his gear.

The gentleman shook his head and went back to reading the sports section. Rylie breathed a sigh of relief and quickly made his exit. The last thing he needed right now was to be recognised.

Where could he lay low for a while and still have access to information? He couldn't go home or to his best friend's place. The authorities would be watching those. He considered calling his friends from Cairns, Joshua and Joey Donnelly. Joshua was in the navy and might be able to help.

He quickly dismissed that idea. They were too far away. What about his pastor? It was worth a try, even though he would probably urge him to go to the police and turn himself in.

"What about Jemma?" Lachlan suggested.

He, Kade and their guest were sitting around the small circular dining table in the open living area.

Deadly Secrets

Kade slid a matter-of-fact glance her way. "Nah, she doesn't look like a Jemma."

She was wolfing down a peanut butter sandwich to his right. Her interested gaze went between the two young men.

Lachlan had not reacted as she had expected when Kade announced they would be having a visitor for a little while. He had calmly shut down his computer and risen from his desk. Although the eyes he trained upon her held a certain measure of distrust, an amused gleam lurked behind them.

He had quipped with a seemingly laid-back attitude, "Kade is always bringing home strays. Last week he wanted to bring home a beached dolphin and I had to convince him the bathtub just wasn't big enough. The time before that it was a possum that'd had a close call with a car, and before that it was an injured magpie."

Kade had levelled him with a dry look and then fallen into easy banter. "You've got to admit, Lachie, that this stray is good looking and may be helpful."

Lachlan had turned and strode toward the kitchen, throwing his answer over his shoulder with a deadpan expression. "I don't know. That possum was awfully cute."

The young woman smiled as she remembered their conversation. She swallowed the last mouthful of her sandwich and returned her attention to her hosts, who were currently attempting to pick out a name for her.

"Paige?"

"As in what you find in a book?" Kade's brows quirked in a telltale 'are you kidding?' expression.

Lachlan's face brightened. "Delta?"

"Like the singer?"

"Jade?"

"Her eyes are blue." Kade studied her unabashed for several seconds. "Well, sort of. They're almost lilac."

She listened wearily to their banter and yawned. "I'll let you call me whatever you want if you'll find me somewhere to sleep." If she closed her eyes right now, she might very well fall asleep at the table.

Both men looked at her and must have noted the exhaustion written all over her face. Kade glanced at Lachlan and grinned mischievously.

"How about Sleepy or Dozy?"

She yawned again. "That just about fits."

Lachlan snorted in amusement and rose noncha-lantly from the table. "I'm going to get my surfing gear." He left Kade the task of settling their guest.

"Come on, sleepy head." Kade stood and waited for her.

She dragged her leaden body out of the chair and

felt the world drastically tilt. Her knees threatened to buckle and she sank back onto the seat. The whole left side of her head was throbbing, with particularly sharp emphasis where it had probably collided with a rock.

She leant upon the table with her elbows to gain some stability. Her left hand hovered over the knot on her skull, desiring to rub the pain away but too afraid to touch the tender area for fear it would make it worse.

"You should be in hospital," Kade stated quietly.

"Why? So they can continue to stuff needles in my arm and tell me what I already know?" She dropped her hand dejectedly onto the tabletop. "It's retrograde amnesia. There's nothing they can do at this point, accept to keep me comfortable and hope that as the swelling on my brain subsides I'll regain my memory."

Kade raised a sceptical brow. "That's what they said?"

"That's the basic gist." She sighed and looked up wearily into the worried face of her host.

Kade studied her in silence, obviously debating what to do. He seemed aware there was more to what the doctor had said than her rudimentary summary. All the same, she would be encouraged to rest while in hospital, which was something she could do right here. He must have come to the same conclusion, for in the next moment, he relaxed.

"We've got a spare bed but it's in the attic. Do you think you can make it up the stairs?" He observed her pale features and drooping eyelids.

"Right now I'd walk over hot coals if I had to." She very slowly got to her feet. She managed to stay upright, keeping her balance by holding onto the edge of the table.

"Okay." Kade's careful tone said that he did not believe her. "Follow me."

With the occasional glance over his shoulder to ensure she was still standing, he led the way up the narrow staircase in the hallway off the living area. Somehow she managed to make it to the attic.

Her fuzzy brain vaguely took in her surroundings, noticing only a dormer window, a door in the far wall and a double bed to its right. "This is nice."

"Yeah." Kade's eyes roamed the room and then rested on its new occupant. "The place belongs to my folks. They had it renovated when they first bought it a few years ago. At the time I think they were intending for it to be a holiday house. Then I moved from Newcastle to Sydney and got a job flying tourists over the harbour. I needed a permanent place to live and they agreed to rent it to me." He shrugged.

"They usually stay in this room when they visit,

which isn't all that often so you won't have to worry about being kicked out any time soon."

She smiled. "Thanks. I really appreciate your kindness."

He held her grateful gaze. "I know you do. Rest up and if you need anything, give me a yell."

"I will." She sat on the edge of the mattress and revelled in its softness. It sure beat what the hospital had to offer.

With a simple nod, he excused himself and disappeared down the stairway. The young woman lifted her legs onto the mattress and let the right side of her face sink into a soft pillow. With a sigh of contentment, her eyelids drifted shut and sleep came swiftly.

Kade paused on the stairway. What if she didn't wake up? Didn't that sometimes happen with head injuries?

'...whosoever has this world's goods, and sees his brother in need, and shuts up his heart from him, how does the love of God abide in him?'

The familiar verse dropped unexpectedly into his thoughts once again.

Okay God, he conceded, *I get the point. We've got a spare bed and she needs one. I just ask that You'll help her to get well and that she'll be alright?*

Peace settled around his heart and he dropped his concerns. If God wasn't worrying, then why should he? He was about to continue down the stairs when he had another thought.

The room had an ensuite, but the towels were in the linen press downstairs. Deciding it couldn't hurt to offer the information, he popped his head around the doorway at the top of the stairs.

He expected to find her looking around her new room, or at the very least sitting where he had left her moments ago. Instead she was curled up on the bedspread fast asleep, too exhausted to bother crawling under the covers.

He stood in the doorway and studied her with a mixture of curiosity and concern. Who was she? Would she really be okay? He concluded it probably wasn't wise to leave her alone in her condition and descended the stairs to inform his housemate of the change in plans for the afternoon.

Lachlan shrugged and dropped onto the couch in the living room. He flicked the television on with a remote control and settled back to watch the cricket.

"Probably just as well. We might have come back to find she'd robbed us blind."

Kade rolled his eyes at his friend's pessimistic remark and flopped into a comfortable recliner, draping a long leg over the arm of the chair. While attempting to watch the cricket match on T.V, his mind was absently pondering the mystery woman sleeping upstairs, and why God had chosen to usher her into their lives.

6

Rylie nervously knocked on his pastor's front door. It was a moderate sized brick home in an estate in Manly, a good twenty minute walk from the beachfront. It also happened to be several blocks away from where his best friend had lived. His heart squeezed painfully with guilt and grief. If it wasn't for him she would still be alive. And if it wasn't for Hayden planting his hard drive in Rylie's laptop case, then none of this would have happened in the first place!

Soft footsteps sounded in the hallway on the other side and the heavy timber door opened. A small, well-rounded woman with short curly hair, wearing a beige skirt and indigo shirt, stood in the entrance. She stared at him with surprised blue eyes.

"Rylie!" Her gaze suddenly clouded with shadows of doubt.

"Hi Mrs. K. Is Pastor Lucas home?" His greeting was subdued. He knew full well why she was astonished at his presence on her doorstep.

"Sure, come in." She stepped aside to allow him

entrance.

"Do you have visitors?" The Kennedy's often had folks over for lunch after church on a Sunday.

She led the way through to the living room. "Not today."

Rylie sighed with relief. He did not need more people knowing his whereabouts than was necessary, especially those whom he could not fully trust. "And the kids?"

He was referring to the middle-aged couple's three children, Elijah who was ten, Esther who was twelve, and their fifteen-year-old, Benjamin.

"They're all at friends' houses." She appeared to easily read his apprehension.

Rylie's heart sank. She had heard the media reports.

"Luke, you have a visitor."

Rylie's gaze went to the large man stretched out on the couch watching a cricket match on television, passionately cheering the Aussies on. He ceased his reprimand of the bowler's nasty spin that bounced straight for the batsman's face, glancing off his helmet. His hazel eyes swung to the doorway. They sobered and his usual warm smile was absent.

He stood to full height, a few inches over six feet. A little weight extended his belly slightly over his khaki shorts and his broad shoulders filled out a trendy t-shirt. With a strong jaw line, sun tanned features and a tattoo on his right arm from his early wild days, he looked nothing like a pastor.

Unsure how he would react, Rylie was slightly intimidated.

His genteel wife gestured for him to enter. "I'll leave you two to talk alone."

Rylie nodded his thanks to her and his gaze followed her briefly when she left. He then returned his attention to the hulk of a man standing with hands on his hips in front of the couch.

Fatherly concern entered Lucas Kennedy's expression. "Son, what took you so long in coming to see me?"

Rylie felt the tight coil in his chest loosen. He could trust this man. "Shock I guess." He shrugged, unable to put into words the horror of the last forty hours.

Lucas nodded toward the armchair next to the couch. "Sit down, Rylie, and tell me what's going on." Compassion edged his tone.

Rylie crossed the burgundy carpet and sank into a well-worn blue armchair against the wall opposite the door. Beside Rylie's chair were a couple of beanbags and a stereo in a low cabinet. A heavy rustic baltic pine coffee table sat in the centre of the room in front of the matching blue couch. Upon the coffee table was a small stack of cooking and gardening magazines, a newspaper and television guide and three empty mugs that had not yet made it to the kitchen sink.

The television was housed by a matching pine cabinet in the corner of the opposite wall, into which was set a floor to ceiling window that looked out onto the front yard. A bookshelf adorned the wall beside the doorway and was laden with texts on a wide variety of subjects, from botany to Biblical theology.

Sitting in front of the top shelf of books was a row of framed pictures of the children. The large framed pictures on the walls were of forests and waterfalls, each scene restful and calling one's mind to reflect on the beauty in creation and its powerful Creator.

Rylie's wandering gaze came to rest upon his pastor, who had taken his seat again. His long legs were stretched before him, his left arm on the armrest and his right along the cushions on the low back of the couch. There in that casual position, he calmly waited for his guest to speak.

Rylie leaned forward in his chair with his elbows on his knees and stared into the relatively new carpet. Where to begin? He was at a complete loss for words. He thought of her and his eyes clouded with tears.

Lucas watched the pain and confusion chase across Rylie's face. The silence stretched and he obviously concluded he would have to draw out the details.

"Son, I think the first thing you need to hear right now is that I don't believe a word of what has been in the news. I know you, Rylie. You have a soft heart that is earnest and steadfast. You're not capable of what I've been hearing." He communicated his sincerity as he made eye contact. "Now, tell me what happened Friday night."

Rylie let out a shaky breath and rubbed his weary face. He felt like he hadn't slept in a week. He swallowed hard against the lump in his throat and began.

"Charlotte and I met up at Circular Quay Friday evening. We were going to spend the weekend whale watching on my parents' boat and decided we'd start with dinner.

"We caught a ferry to Watson's bay where we bought fish and chips at Doyle's. It's her favourite. We finished eating and had about half an hour till the next ferry to Manly arrived, and so we went for a walk along the cliffs for something to do.

"I'm a little sketchy on what happened next. Someone clubbed me from behind and I hit the pavement pretty hard. I remember her screaming my name and hearing a scuffle. Then it all went quiet and a voice I'll never forget spoke into my ear. He said if I didn't give him what he wanted, he would throw her over the cliff. I told him I didn't know what he was talking about and he said, 'have it your way'.

"I heard her call my name again, but this time it wasn't as strong and it sounded strange. I tried to get up but I must have passed out because I don't remember anything else."

Rylie paused, willing himself to go on. Tears now ran down his cheeks in rivulets and he wiped them away. "I woke up tied to a chair in pitch-black darkness and I heard that voice again. He hit me a few times trying to get information. Something about Hayden's external hard drive. I had no idea what he was talking about. He said that just before he had killed Hayden, Hayden had admitted that he had stashed it in my laptop case.

"Eventually he left and I sat there in darkness for hours wondering what on earth was going on. I'm guessing now he used that time to frame me for Hayden's death.

"Anyway, by the grace of God, I managed to get free and I crawled out of an air vent. I found then that he'd been holding me in one of the tunnels at the gun emplacement at South Head. I found the closest house to use an old lady's phone. I was about to call the police when the news came on and I saw that I had been blamed for Hayden's death. I figured it had something to do with Hayden's external hard drive.

"I'd accidentally left my laptop on the ferry and after some running around I managed to get it back. The hard drive was there alright. I hadn't even known he had stashed it on me.

"Anyway, today I took a look at what was on it and I just can't work it out. He's been collecting files and data from places I don't want to know how he accessed. I can't figure out how they're all connected or why he would want them."

Rylie leaned back in the chair, totally exhausted in every way.

A puzzled frown knit Lucas' brow. "Maybe the authorities can help?"

"I thought you might say something like that." Rylie sighed and ran a hand through his hair and rested his head against the back of the chair. "The only problem with that idea is they think I killed Hayden. Whoever kidnapped me and killed Charlotte must have planted something of mine at the crime scene."

"The newspapers say Hayden was killed in the botanic gardens around the same time you were in Watson's Bay with Charlotte. You have an alibi."

Tears blurred Rylie's vision. "Not anymore I don't. The cliff, remember?"

Lucas' eyes lit with discovery. "Maybe you do."

Rylie raised his head from the chair and stared at his pastor in bewilderment. "Who?"

Looking like a man on a mission, his pastor headed for the doorway. "Hang on a minute." He tossed this over his shoulder and strode toward the kitchen.

Rylie could hear his voice from the living room.

"Emmy, where's this morning's paper?"

"In the recycle bin. You said you had finished with it." A hint of confusion tinged Emeline Kennedy's reply.

Rylie waited another five minutes for his pastor to return. The man finally marched into the room with a crumpled paper in his hands that he had dug out of the bin. He pulled the coffee table closer, dropped the paper onto its cluttered surface and sat on the edge of the couch. With brow furrowed in concentration, he flipped through the pages looking for something specific. He was halfway through when he tapped an article and smiled triumphantly.

"Check this out, son." He passed the newspaper to Rylie who was now sitting forward in the armchair. "It's the one at the bottom on the left. It's only small, but it may just be what we need."

He pointed to the spot as Rylie took the paper. It was entitled, 'Mystery woman found by joggers.' He began to read.

'A young woman, presumably in her early twenties, was spotted by two joggers washed up on the rocks below the South Head Saturday morning. She was rescued by a police boat and taken by

ambulance to hospital, where she is currently in
a stable condition, but is suffering amnesia due
to a serious head injury.'

Rylie did not finish reading. He glanced up at Lucas
and felt hope burgeon within him. "Are you saying
that it's possible she's alive?"

Lucas raised his brows in an expression that said
it was likely. "This woman was found where you and
Charlotte were attacked. She probably *was* thrown
over the cliff and ended up being washed onto the
rocks. It's a miracle she even survived. Read on, they
describe what she looks like."

'Police have asked for people to come forward
who may be able to help establish her identity
and the circumstances surrounding her discovery at the base of the cliffs. The mystery woman
is roughly five foot and nine inches with blue
eyes and long brown hair. She was wearing black
shorts and a purple t-shirt.'

Rylie's eyes widened in astonishment and his heart
leapt with joy. "That's her! Pastor Luke, Charlie was
wearing black shorts and a purple t-shirt that night!
She's alive! I've got to find her."

"Does it say which hospital they took her to? I can't
remember."

Rylie scanned the rest of the article and frowned.
"No. Privacy laws I guess."

Lucas grinned. "All the same, she's alive. Now you
can go to the authorities and tell them your side of

the story and she can confirm it."

Disappointment came crashing down around Rylie. "No, she can't. It says here she has amnesia due to a head injury. She's not going to remember what happened and it's likely she won't even remember me."

Lucas tented his fingers before him pensively. "Well," he finally concluded optimistically, "you'll never know until you try."

Rylie sat quietly, pondering how he could possibly trace her whereabouts. He could try going to the various hospitals in Sydney, but then he did not want to be recognised, so that was not really an option. He could send Lucas to look for her. That was more sensible. The seed of an idea dropped into his thoughts and began to germinate.

Wait a minute! A slow smile began to cross his face. *Her cell phone has GPS.*

He quickly stood. "Pastor Luke, can I use your computer? It's hooked to the net right?"

Lucas frowned in puzzlement and shrugged. "Sure. Benjamin uses it to research assignments for school."

"Broadband?"

"Yeah. What are you thinking of doing?"

Rylie strode from the room. "Come with me and I'll show you."

7

The young woman stood at the kitchen counter in the morning and read the note sitting next to a half eaten loaf of bread. Beside it a peanut butter jar was still open with a knife standing up inside.

'To Lela,

I have decided to call you that after my favourite rabbit when I was a kid. She had big blue eyes. I hope you do not run away too. She dug under her cage and I never saw her again. I was crushed.'

She chuckled. He was incorrigible! She read on.

'Lachie and me have gone to work. We will be back in time for dinner, which will probably be peanut butter sandwiches again unless Lachie remembers to go to the store. We will see you tonight. Take it easy and look after yourself.

Kade.

P.S Don't chew on any shoes or furniture like the original Lela. There's bread on the counter in case you get hungry.'

She shook her head at his quirky sense of humour and tried the name on her tongue. "Lela." It would do for now.

She let her gaze wander over the kitchen and then the open living space. The floor throughout the house was of hardwood. The kitchen had been made over in the same rich tones, with spacious highly glossed benches, range hood and cupboards. Sleek steel appliances such as a kettle, toaster, dishwasher, stove and a large refrigerator made it functional.

However, the sink was piled high with pots and pans and the benches looked like they had never been introduced to a sponge. The floor was covered with dust and crumbs, and dirty plates, utensils, bowls and cups had not quite made it to the dishwasher. Her focus shifted to the circular table just beyond the kitchen counter in the dining area. It was a lovely piece of furniture that had also been badly neglected.

She surveyed the remnants of several dinners cleaving to the tabletop. "It's a wonder the ants haven't taken over this place."

She turned her attention to the lounge suite on the left of the living space. A red suede couch and a matching armchair took pride of place in the centre, facing the wall which the door opened against. Sitting alongside the cream plaster was a low chic black television cabinet with a huge plasma screen on display. Through the glass of the cabinet she could see a

DVD player and a play station. Positioned around the room were speakers to provide surround sound.

"Boys and their toys."

Her eyes drifted to the computer desk. It was the one tidy space in the whole room. Pens were neatly contained in a tin. Other stationery items were hidden from view in a set of draws. A computer occupied the top of the workspace, and if one looked past the screen, they could easily view the pristine sand and rich blue water of the cove.

She smiled in amusement. It was obvious who the neat person in the house was and who made the majority of mess. She wondered how Lachlan tolerated Kade's disarray and finally concluded that he had probably given up cleaning after him when it became obvious he wasn't about to lift his game any time soon.

"I don't blame you, Lachie. How about I give you a great big thank you for putting up with a total stranger by cleaning this place up?"

Lela wasn't feeling one hundred percent yet, but at least the dizziness had subsided. She made herself a peanut butter sandwich and quickly ate. Then she hastily went about setting the house in order.

* * *

"It has no signal, which means she's still got it and it's waterlogged, or it fell out of her pocket and is lying at the bottom of the ocean."

Rylie's attempt to track Charlotte's position by tracing her cell phone had failed. He shut the Kennedy's computer down.

Lucas wandered to the window of the study. "It was worth a try." He looked out over the backyard absently.

"What now?"

Lucas turned to face him. "I think you should turn yourself in. Let the police find her." He leaned against the windowsill and held Rylie's gaze.

"She's still in danger. Whoever came after us will realise they've failed and try again."

Lucas studied him quietly. Rylie could make a pretty good guess what he was planning on doing. There was no other legal solution.

"This is what I'm going to do."

Lucas waited patiently.

"I want you to turn me in."

A half smile tugged at the pastor's lips. "I was going to."

"When you call the police, tell them what I've told you, every detail. Then I want you to start looking in all the hospitals around Sydney for Charlotte. I can't, but you can."

"Smart move, son. If someone is truly after you, then you will be safer in police custody."

"You're probably right."

"Let's pray first."

"Heaven knows I need it." Rylie bowed his head.

The pastor's large hand rested on his shoulder and his steady voice began an earnest prayer.

"Father God, I ask your special protection for Rylie right now. Please help us all to get to the bottom of the situation speedily, and please help the authorities to clear his name? Show them who is really to blame for Hayden's death? Please comfort Hayden's family and we ask that you will bring Charlotte safely home again? We pray all of this in the name of Jesus."

"Amen." Rylie looked up into the big man's eyes and smiled resignedly. "Go make the call."

Lucas gave his shoulder a squeeze and smiled sadly. He clearly hated to phone the police, especially when he knew Rylie was innocent, but it was the honest thing to do.

He strode from the room and Rylie snatched up his laptop. He swung its strap over his head and shoulder, gently opened the window and quietly slipped from the house.

He'd had no intention of turning himself in for the simple reason that whatever 'hard evidence' had been found would mean that nobody would take him seriously. He would be of more use to Charlotte if he was free and able to continue sifting through Hayden's hard drive to find the guilty culprit and his motive.

As he snuck out the back gate and disappeared onto the streets of Manly, he felt bad about deceiving Pastor Lucas. He consoled himself that it was better this way. At least his pastor would have plausible deniability and the man had not abetted a criminal. Hopefully it would also start the police searching a little deeper for answers, and this time in the right places.

Kade did not know what had possessed him to return to the cliffs. Perhaps it was in the vain hope that he might find something to help Lela discover her identity. Whatever it was that had prompted him, now urged him to do a more thorough search of the area.

He had knocked off work over an hour ago and was now running a whole lot later than he had expected, and daylight was fast receding. He wondered if she would still be there when he returned. Something told him she would.

He was about to give up the fruitless search, when

the last rays of sunlight glinted off something beneath a shrub near the fence. Kade took a few steps closer, crouched down and retrieved it.

He turned the mobile phone over in his hands, noticing that it had spatters of blood on the buttons and the screen. He wondered if it was Lela's. It was highly likely considering where he had found it and that it was bloody. Had she hit her head before falling, or had she been attacked and thrown over the cliff?

The sun sank further below the horizon, peering over enough to offer the earth one last orange wink before it disappeared altogether. Kade stood and glanced down at the phone in his hand, his mind working over the various possibilities. All of them left a bitter taste in his mouth.

Deciding his best bet was to discuss the matter with Lachlan and Lela, he fetched his bike from the old hotel. He regularly chained it there in the mornings before catching the ferry to work. He hopped on and powered home, driven by a host of questions with no immediate answers.

8

"Okay, read it to me," Lachlan urged as he sat at his computer desk.

Lela glanced at the landline beneath the word 'home' in the contacts section of the mobile and read it aloud. She then watched as Lachlan's fingers tapped away at the keys and he intermittently moved the mouse at lightning speed.

"What are you doing?"

"I'm tracing the address of that phone number. If the cell is truly yours, then we'll be able to find where you live." His eyes remained glued to the screen.

Her brows rose in surprise. "You can do that?"

He shrugged. "Sure."

Lela bit her lower lip. Anything to do with the computer was over her head.

Well, at least now you know you're not a computer nerd.

"What have you done?" came Kade's disillusioned cry from his bedroom. "I can't find anything!"

"What's new?" Lachlan shot back.

Kade appeared in the doorway to the living room.

"She's cleaned everything, even my room. It's an invasion of my personal space!"

Lela smiled at him in amusement and then returned her focus to Lachlan and the computer screen.

"Doesn't anyone care that she's turned my happy, contented world upside down?"

Kade received absolutely no pity.

"I for one wish she'd move in permanently and you would move out," Lachlan teased with a deadpan. "She's the cleanest roomy I've ever had."

Kade looked mildly offended. "Are you serious?"

Lachlan grinned at him over his shoulder. "I don't know. She cleaned the toilet and used fabric softener on the towels. She vacuums, mops and scrubs and she even-"

"Yeah, I get the picture." Kade waved his hand. It was a losing battle and he obviously knew it.

Lachlan drew up the information he wanted. He hit the print screen button. "Got it." He snatched the printout of an address and passed it to Lela.

"Got what?" Kade wandered into the room. He glanced at the sheet of paper over Lela's shoulder and then at his friend. "Is this where she lives?"

"Maybe. It all depends on whether this is her phone or not." He took it from her fingers and held it up.

Lela marvelled that he had come up with an address so quickly.

"How do you do stuff like that? I mean, it's a little scary. You could track down just about anyone with that thing." Kade pointed at the computer whirring softly on the desk.

Lachlan took his jacket off the back of his desk chair. He thrust his arms in and shrugged it on. "Probably. Let's go."

"Where?" Kade appeared to be left behind in the conversation.

Lela smiled. His mind was likely still reeling from the fact that the house was spotlessly clean. Lachlan rolled his eyes and Lela spelled it out for him.

"We're going to this address to see if it's where I live. Hopefully we'll get some answers."

"Oh," Kade answered rather sheepishly. "Where are my windcheaters?"

"In your drawers like they should be."

Looking suitably chastised and somewhat mothered, he went to find some warmer clothes while Lachlan shut down the computer.

He knew it was wrong, but he was running out of options. Rylie found a secluded spot in someone's front yard and connected to their wireless internet. It was the only one out of the last three his computer had detected that was not password protected.

He searched for Charlotte's mobile signal as he had done at the Kennedy's and was pleased beyond measure when his laptop picked it up. He used her GPS signal and was able to track the cell's position on a map of Sydney. His brows shot up in surprise.

The phone was currently travelling across the harbour toward Manly. Whoever had it was coming to him. He checked his laptop battery and was satisfied that it would hold out for at least another two hours. Good. He would sit and wait and track where her phone was going.

He prayed desperately that it was in her possession and that tonight he would finally see her face to face.

"Are you sure this is the place?" Kade asked the two standing beside him.

They were on the sidewalk in a suburban area not far from the seashore, staring up at a three-storey brick apartment building.

Lachlan glanced at the address on the paper in Lela's hand and then back at the structure before them. It was far from glamorous and it was quite dated, however it did appear to be well kept and the area felt safe. "Yeah, this is it."

"How do we get inside?"

Lachlan turned to Lela. "Did you have any keys on you when you were discovered on Saturday?"

She shook her head.

Lachlan frowned. "Okay. I guess we need to come up with another way in. Kade, got any ideas?"

"What about those?" He pointed toward the small balconies along the north side of the building at each level. Some were cluttered with junk or had washing hanging out to dry on racks. The first one had an outdoor setting suitable for eating a leisurely breakfast in the fresh air.

Lachlan looked surprised that his friend had come up with a logical solution. "That might work. The address says apartment one, so let's try the lower balcony."

The land sloped downward on that side, which meant that the balcony was at least three metres from the ground. They stood beneath it and assessed the situation.

Kade stared up at their destination. "Lachie, give me a boost."

Lachlan groaned and reluctantly complied. Kade was no lightweight. He was over six feet of solid muscle. Nevertheless, he linked his hands together, gritted his teeth and boosted his friend.

Kade's hands grasped the balcony ledge and he pulled himself up and over. With a quick look through the flywire screen to ensure there was nobody inside about to get the fright of their life, he reached down over the balcony and offered his hand.

"Alright, Lela, up you come."

Lachlan rolled his eyes and performed the task again. Lela was slightly taller than him and yet thankfully much lighter than Kade. He grasped her hand as Lachlan boosted her up and pulled her the rest of the way. He reached back down again.

"Alright, your return Lachie. Jump."

Lachlan sent him a frustrated glare.

"Come on, you can do it."

Lachlan sighed and gave in. He crouched down and then swung his arms upward and leapt. He missed Kade's fingers by an inch.

"Hurry before someone sees!" Kade hissed.

"It's easy for you to say!" he retorted in a sharp whisper. "You had help."

Lela chuckled softly and Kade passed her a cheeky grin. Lachlan geared up and tried again. This time Kade's hand firmly grasped his wrist. With much struggling and grunting between the two of them, Lachlan managed to climb onto the balcony. They moved into the shadow of an alcove and surveyed the door.

Kade grinned. "You beauty! The wire screen is locked but the latch on the glass door isn't secured." He whipped a pocketknife from a zip pocket in his cargo pants and flicked open the blade.

Lachlan passed him a dry look. "Aren't you just the regular action man."

Lela glanced nervously over the street. "Do you realise you're breaking and entering?"

"Not if it's your house."

Kade's logical perspective failed to reassure her. "She's right. Hurry up."

"I am." Kade inserted the blade and slit the flywire near the latch. He reached his fingers in and flicked the screen lock. "How about that guys?" He smiled mischievously and slid the door back. "Breaking and entering, a quick lesson by Kade Haynes."

"Whatever, just get in!" Lachlan impatiently shoved his friend through the doorway.

Lela chuckled and followed them. It was dark and not even the street lamps outside provided illumination. She drew the curtains either side of the balcony closed and felt around the walls until she came across a light switch. She flicked it on and the room came into full view. Her heart leapt into her throat and her hand covered her mouth. Kade exhaled a troubled breath.

"Wow, even you couldn't mess up a house this badly." Lachlan directed this comment at his house-mate.

"You got that right." Kade studied the chaos that had once been a living room.

The apartment had been ransacked. A bookshelf had been tipped over and books and DVDs were scattered across the floor. The couch had been torn to shreds, or rather deliberately cut and the stuffing pulled out as though someone had been looking for something hidden inside. Cushions had been disem-bowelled, the contents of a TV cabinet were strewn across the floor, and papers from a desk against the far wall littered the room as though a mighty gust of wind had blown through.

The kitchen off the living room had every cupboard open with packets of food tossed haphazardly onto the floor. Broken glasses, bowls, plates and utensils were added to the disarray. Whoever had trashed the apartment had left nothing untouched.

"If this was thieves then the TV, DVD player and computer over there would be gone. Whoever did this was looking for something," Lachlan observed soberly.

A chill ran down Lela's spine. She was coming to the same conclusions as her new friends. She had something someone wanted, and ending up at the bottom of that cliff had been no accident. That is, if this really was her apartment. She felt nothing. No sense of connection or familiarity. It might not belong to her after all.

Kade reached down into the rubble and drew forth a photograph from a shattered picture frame. He examined it quietly and then wordlessly passed it to Lachlan. He glanced at it and then at Lela.

Concern over their solemn expressions mounted. "What is it?"

Lachlan handed it to her. He answered as she scrutinized the picture. "It's you. It looks like it was taken recently at the Sydney Tower. See, you're both in skywalk suits."

Lela inspected the two subjects in blue and yellow jump suits and harnesses set against the Sydney skyline. The first smiling face was hers and it was familiar only because she had looked at it in the mirror that morning. The other was a young man roughly the same age as her.

He had an arm around her shoulders and she had one around his. His eyes were sea green and his short hair was blond. He was most definitely good looking, although not as solid in frame as Kade. He resembled Lachlan's trim build.

"Who is he?"

"Your brother?" Kade suggested with a hopeful

gleam in his eyes.

"More like her boyfriend."

"Hang on a minute." Kade snatched the photograph back and studied the man with Lela. "I've seen this guy before."

Lachlan frowned and took a closer look at the picture. "Where?"

"On the news last night. I didn't think anything of it till now." Kade's troubled gaze met theirs. "Guys, this bloke killed a man in the Sydney botanic gardens a couple of days ago."

9

When Rylie was certain the cell phone was stationary, he packed up his laptop and jogged to its last known location. He knew exactly where it was. Charlotte's apartment.

It was a ten minute run and he arrived two houses down where he stopped to catch his breath.

He adjusted his laptop case which was slung over his shoulder and carefully studied the street. He was about to precede when a black sports car pulled to the curb outside the large brick building, and a man in his late twenties to early thirties unfolded from behind the steering wheel.

Rylie stepped into the shadow of a tall jacaranda on the nature strip and observed him in the partial light. He was of medium height and was solidly built. He wore trendy denim jeans and a hooded windcheater, and as he closed the car door he tucked a dark, L-shaped object into the back of his waistband.

Rylie's eyes widened in alarm. It was a pistol. His frightened gaze swung to the lower balcony where a sliver of light was showing from behind drawn curtains. It then returned to the man steadfastly approaching the front door of the building. He produced a key from his back pocket and opened the security door.

He was about to go in when the telltale noise of a mobile phone broke the stillness of the evening. He fished a cell from his pocket, the sound growing louder when it was able to drift on the gentle breeze. Rylie could easily hear his side of the conversation.

"Yes. Her signal says she's here. It won't take more than a minute. ... I won't botch it up. I don't know how she survived the last time. Just dumb luck I guess. ... Yes boss. ... Yes I know." The man continued to talk on the front stoop and a shiver went down Rylie's spine.

He would recognise that voice anywhere. It was his kidnapper and the man who had attempted to kill Charlotte!

Rylie whipped out his phone from his laptop case and turned it on. Up till now he had not been game to use it for fear the authorities would trace his location. Now that seemed insignificant. He dialled Charlotte's number and waited an interminable fifteen seconds before someone answered. It was a male voice.

"Hello?"

Rylie wasted no time. "Is she there with you?"

Confusion laced the reply. "Who is this?"

"A friend. Look, she's tall, has brown hair, lilac eyes. Is she there with you?"

"Whoever you are, you're creeping me out." Now the voice held suspicion.

The kidnapper ended his conversation. He reached for the handle and opened the door.

"Look, I haven't got time to explain. You're in danger. There's a guy coming in the front door and he's got a gun. Get out. Get out now!"

"What in the-"

"Go out through the balcony door! Hurry!" He shut off his phone. However, the authorities would no doubt swarm the place in minutes anyway. He had to act quickly to buy them all some time.

Rylie ran to the car, crouched by a back tyre and unscrewed the air cap. He held the centrepiece down and it began to deflate.

Lachlan listened to the dial tone on Lela's phone in stunned silence and then disconnected.

Kade noted his friend's uneasiness. "What was that about?"

"It was-" Lachlan froze mid sentence and his eyes widened in alarm as the front door handle across the room jiggled ever so gently.

He leapt across the debris on the floor and turned the deadbolt with suddenly shaky fingers. "Get out!" he whispered furiously at Kade and Lela who were watching him with concern.

Lela was the first to move into action. She turned for the balcony doorway and slipped outside. Kade followed her and Lachlan was only a step behind. Lela swung her legs over the brick barrier and jumped. She landed on her feet as agile as a cat and bolted for the next-door neighbour's garden.

Kade was hot on her heels. Lachlan jumped last and sprinted after his comrades. He scaled the neighbour's fence and crouched behind a row of lavender bushes. Then they heard a masculine voice out the front of the building curse angrily.

Kade peered over the shrubbery to see what was going on. A dark figure emerged from the building and ran toward his car that was rolling down the street. Another man, clearly the guilty culprit who had taken off the handbrake, gave the vehicle one last push down the incline before turning and bolting in the opposite direction.

The villain raised his right arm level with the escapee and Kade was stunned to see a gun clutched in his hand. A shot rang out and the guy who had caused the diversion twisted mid stride and fell hard against the pavement.

The gunman then tore after his sports car. It was steadily picking up speed and heading straight for a house on the street running across the intersection at the bottom of the slope.

Without thinking his actions through, Kade leapt over the fence again and darted across the road to the footpath on the opposite side. He grabbed the downed man roughly by the right arm and hauled him to his feet. Kade's gaze followed the gunman who dove into his car and jammed on the handbrake. They did not have much time.

The injured man groaned and clutched at his left arm. He appeared as though he would collapse. Suddenly Lachlan was there practically dragging him down the footpath.

The young man resisted. "My laptop!"

Lela, who had followed Lachlan, slung the case that had hit the pavement over her shoulder and chased after him. With one last glance at their attacker, who was now starting his vehicle, Kade followed.

They rounded a bend out of sight and kept running. They came to another corner and the sound of a V8 engine rumbling in the distance spurred them onward. They had travelled to Manly on the ferry, which unfortunately was likely be the first place the gunman would look.

Lachlan dove into another front yard and dropped down behind a thick hedge that was roughly the height of his hips. Kade and Lela crouched beside them. The wounded man dropped to his knees. He was breathing hard. In the darkness it was difficult to see his face.

"What if he finds us here?" Kade asked the question they were all likely thinking.

"He won't be going far," the injured man said with a grin. "I let the air out of his back tyre. He'll need to stop and pump it up or he'll lose control if he drives any faster than fifty."

Kade chuckled and clapped him on the back. "Thanks mate. I dunno who you are or where you came from, but I'm sure glad you were around."

"Sh!" Lela hissed as the burble of a V8 drew closer. She peered around the corner of the hedge. She spotted the black sports car driving slowly up the street toward them and quickly withdrew into the shadows.

A police siren wailed in the distance and grew steadily louder. The black sports car cruised past, and the driver must have heard the siren, for he planted his foot on the accelerator. The car fishtailed and he was forced to slow down or lose control. It limped around a bend out of sight and the four individuals hiding behind the hedge sagged with relief.

Lachlan stood. "Come on, let's get out of here."

The injured man got to his feet. Blood seeped between the fingers clutching his left arm. Light from a nearby street lamp illuminated his face for the first time and all three bystanders were shocked.

"It's you!" Kade glared at the twenty-year-old. "You're the murderer from the news!"

"My name is Rylie Hunter and I'm not a murderer." Irritation was written all over his face. "The same guy that came after you back there nearly killed me, and her." He nodded toward Lela who was staring at him in a stunned stupor. "He also killed Hayden and framed me for his death."

"Yeah right!" Lachlan flipped open Lela's cell phone to call the police.

"I'd turn that thing off if I was you," Rylie warned. "That's how he found you. He traced your signal using your GPS."

Lachlan pulled the phone away from his ear and stared at it as though it had grown horns. He quickly turned it off. "Don't think I'm not going to turn you in!"

Rylie rolled his eyes heavenward. "Oh for crying out loud! If I was a murderer, would I have helped you back there? I could have let that guy kill you, but I didn't."

Kade eyed the fugitive from head to toe. "He's got

a point, and he looks harmless enough."

"Tell that to the dead guy in the botanic gardens!"

"Would all of you pipe down?" Lela slashed downward with her hands in frustration. "A man just came after us and you're standing here debating over whether *he* is a threat!" She pointed at Rylie and then cast Lachlan and Kade an irate glare. "Let's just get him to a doctor and then we'll sort this out."

"No! I can't see a doctor. If I do, the police will find me and then so will whoever it is that wants me dead. I'll be okay. It's just a flesh wound."

Kade's right brow winged upward sceptically. "Mate, you're losing blood like a leaky tap."

"I don't care. Let's just get her somewhere safe." He held Lela's level gaze and Kade observed that there seemed to be a bond. He had cared about her enough to risk his own life.

"Let's take him home," she suggested to the boys.

Lachlan nearly exploded. "Are you serious?"

Rylie, Kade and Lela simultaneously hushed him.

He lowered his voice. "Are you serious? He's a criminal!"

"Kade, Lachie says you're a sucker for injured things. You've already got one stray, why not another?"

Kade opened his mouth to argue, then closed it as a familiar verse floated through his mind.

'... whosoever has this world's goods, and sees his brother in need, and shuts up his heart from him, how does the love of God abide in him?'

Yeah, but this isn't smart God.

'How does the love of God abide in him?'

He growled under his breath and conceded defeat. "Okay, but only for tonight."

Lachlan just shook his head. Meanwhile Lela gave a satisfied nod.

"Good. Now, how do we get home without being seen? The ferry will be the first place he'll look for us. He knows we're on foot."

"No worries," Rylie chipped into the conversation. "My parents have a boat down at the mariner. It'll take us anywhere we want to go."

"Great!" Lachlan threw his hands up in the air. "Now we're adding theft to breaking and entering!"

"It's not stealing." Rylie peered around the hedge. He glanced up and down the street.

The police cars had driven out of sight and were likely at her apartment, probably due to an emergency phone call by a neighbour hearing the gunshot, or maybe they had tracked a cell phone. Either way, Kade did not want to hang around.

"My folks let me use it whenever I like."

"Yeah, but we're still aiding and abetting a criminal!"

"I'm not a criminal. I've been framed." He took one more look at the empty street. "The coast is clear. Let's go. The marina is that way." He pointed west.

Lachlan muttered under his breath. All the same, he followed the three as they wove through the backstreets of Manly toward the water.

10

"This was the location he phoned from," Detective Constable Tiana Dalsanto informed her colleague.

Detective Sergeant Bodhi Lazzaro pulled the unmarked vehicle to the curb outside an apartment building in Manly. The pair quietly assessed the scene before them. Two squad cars were parked nearby and the street had been cordoned off. Police officers were talking to witnesses who had come from neighbouring houses, gleaning information regarding the shooting that had taken place half an hour ago.

In unspoken agreement, the pair got out of the vehicle. Bodhi was at least two heads taller than Tiana and a good ten years older. At thirty-seven, he did not consider himself old by a long shot. Yet somehow the new detectives seemed to be getting younger and younger.

Tiana did not look in the least bit like a police officer. She was short, cute and spunky with large puppy dog eyes and long straight black hair braided down her back. He often remarked cheekily that her utility belt weighed more than she did. In a fight he would rather a male officer by his side, however in investigation situations such as this, Tiana had proven herself invaluable.

"So the question is, was Rylie Hunter the one doing the shooting, and if so, who was he shooting at?" Bodhi mused aloud.

"There's a patch of what looks like blood spatter on the pavement just there." Tiana pointed to an area that was being photographed by a fellow policeman.

"Neighbours reported a break-in in apartment one. I'll check that out and chat with the officer in charge while you gather DNA."

"Mmm." She sounded preoccupied. Her mind was already on the case and her sharp eyes were taking in every detail on the now busy, lamp lit street. Bodhi smiled and left her to it.

Rylie sat on the closed toilet lid as he was directed, while the woman they called Lela gathered disinfectant and bandages from the washbasin cupboard. He leaned back against the toilet water tank and blinked to clear his vision. It didn't work. He still felt lightheaded and the occasional black spot danced before his eyes. He guessed it was from loss of blood. He was also shaking from head to foot. Shock had arrived in full force.

He caught movement from the corner of his eye and glanced up at the doorway. Lachlan was standing there, hands on his hips, observing him with an unreadable expression.

Rylie had explained what had happened in detail on their journey across the harbour in his parents' small luxury yacht. It looked more like a sleek jet boat, and yet beneath the deck was a tiny galley, bathroom and sleeping quarters.

Kade had drooled over the vessel, and without needing an invitation, had taken the helm. He had dropped them off at the cove and driven the boat to a private jetty nearby that was owned by a friend. He had planned to jog home and Rylie figured he was probably not far away by now.

"So where is this external hard drive you talked about?" Lachlan's expression held a good measure of both scepticism and challenge.

Lela glanced at her new housemate. "I left his laptop by the front door."

Lachlan eyed Rylie suspiciously. "I'll take a look at it." He cast one last distrustful glance at the wounded man before leaving them alone.

Lela turned from the first aid items she had laid beside the sink and wordlessly lifted Rylie's jumper over his head. He was too weak and exhausted to do anything but comply. His arm lodged a severe protest, however the biggest response he could muster was a sharp intake of breath.

"You think that hurts?" She tossed his blood soaked windcheater in the bathtub. "Just wait till I get at that bullet hole with some disinfectant."

He smiled feebly. "Do what you have to." He clenched his teeth in anticipation.

She took his arm in her right hand and inspected the entrance and exit holes. Thanks to Lachlan's reluctant intervention on the boat ride, the bleeding had stopped.

He had wrapped it in a towel from below deck and held the injured arm up over Rylie's head. Between the pressure of the towel, Lachlan's grip and the elevation, the blood flow had dribbled down to nothing in a relatively short time.

"I think you were right about this being just a flesh wound. I don't think it's gone through the bone." Lela seemed totally unaffected by the gruesome sight.

He thought on her chosen profession and had to agree that it suited her. She had the stomach for just about anything.

"It could do with some stitches."

"Unless you're willing to do those yourself, I'll have to live without." He studied her intently while she worked to clean up his arm. He was amazed that she did not know him. She really did have amnesia. A weight of sadness settled over him. She had lost the years of camaraderie and friendship. The memories, the fun, the laughter, the tears; it was all gone.

"What are you looking at?" Her eyes never left the bandage she was carefully wrapping around his arm.

"You."

She said nothing. She silently finished her ministrations and disposed of the bloody cloth she had used to mop up the mess. She tossed his windcheater into the bin beside the cupboard and wiped the soiled surface.

He eyed the excellent job she had done on the bandage. "Thanks Charlie."

Her gaze snapped to meet his. "Who is that?"

He held eye contact. "It's you."

She looked into his gentle sea green eyes and her features softened with sisterly affection. "Charlie is a boy's name."

He smiled warmly. "It's short for Charlotte."

Her lips tugged at the corners. "How do you know me?"

Rylie's heart squeezed painfully in his chest over the innocent query. "We've been best friends for four years."

She seemed to read the sadness in his eyes. "Are we... Have we ever..."

Knowing her well, Rylie was able to guess the direction her thoughts had travelled. He smiled warmly in amusement. "No. We've never dated. We talked about getting serious with each other when you moved to Sydney a year ago, and we both decided it would be a big mistake. We've always been good friends. It would have been like dating a sibling."

He could see she found him intriguing. Whether it was his reference to God, or the kindness in his expression, the gentle way he spoke to her, or his usual open honesty, he wasn't sure. But she liked him, of that he was positive.

"Thanks for telling me. It must be hard being treated as a stranger."

An affectionate light sparkled in his weary eyes. "You're not a stranger to me. Even without your memory, you haven't changed a bit. It's so good to know you're alright."

She smiled with delight, obviously touched by the sincere remark.

"How's the stray, Lela?"

Kade had picked up only the last bit of conversation and made a few deductions, one of which was unexpectedly disturbing. He scrutinised the fugitive, hoping for Lela's sake he was what he claimed to be. If he was guilty, then she was in for a lot of heartache.

He might also be the biggest con-artist on the planet and turn out to be the one who had pushed her over the cliff. Kade was hesitant to trust him and found himself feeling protective.

She passed him a friendly smile. "It's Charlotte apparently, and he's doing fine."

"Charlotte hey?" Kade studied her face and a teasing gleam entered his cheeky brown eyes. "Nah, you still look like a Lela to me."

"You can call me whatever you want," she replied nonchalantly, "just as long as it's not Rover."

Rylie's face screwed up in confusion. "Rover?"

She and Kade exchanged amused glances.

"It's an ongoing joke." She frowned at Rylie. "You look exhausted." She turned to her new friend. "Kade, where can we put him?"

Kade shrugged. "The couch?"

"Compared to where I've been sleeping, a couch sounds heavenly." Rylie's tone was dry.

He rose to his feet and his blood pressure must have dropped. His knees buckled and he went down, landing hard on the closed toilet lid. Kade and Charlotte both made a grab for him before he could topple into the bathtub.

"Whoa!" Kade pushed Rylie's limp body back against the toilet tank. "Stay with us buddy."

He saw the injured man's eyes begin to roll as though he would pass out. He seemed to come out of it and shook his head.

"Are you okay?" Charlotte asked worriedly.

"Which one of you tipped the room on its end?" he attempted a joke and fought to remain conscious.

"It was her." Kade nodded toward Charlotte with a deadpan. "She has a way of turning a man's world upside down." He gave her a teasing look as he re-membered her massive cleanup that day.

"Nothing new there."

Something inside Kade wilted in disappointment at Rylie's quip. This man spoke as though he knew her intimately, and in light of the photograph in her apartment, he probably did. Kade shelved his con-cerns and turned to business.

"Lela... I mean Charlotte, help me get him to his feet?"

"Sure."

They both pulled, and with each under an arm, managed to get him upright. His knees buckled again and this time he did pass out. Kade manoeuvred Rylie's deadweight and hefted him over his shoulder.

Charlotte followed them into the hallway and looked inquisitively at Kade when he did not head for the living room but instead turned right. He laid the unconscious man on his own bed and placed a pillow under his shoulders so that his head rolled back, keeping his airway open.

"Why are you putting him in here?"

Kade stared at the injured man. "Whoever has this world's goods," he muttered and ran a hand through his curly sun bleached hair.

Charlotte frowned in bewilderment. "Pardon?"

Kade sighed and waved in dismissal. "Never mind. Will you keep an eye on him while I go see what Lachie is up to? He was doing something clever on his computer when I wandered through a few minutes ago. Beats me what he's up to."

"Yeah." She watched him go with a puzzled crease between her brows.

11

Charlotte awoke from a nightmare with a start and sat bolt upright. The image of a dark skinned man with vivid blue eyes, holding her hostage in a zodiac, was burned into her memory. The feel of his strong arms around her collarbone as he used her as a human shield from automatic gunfire, sent a shiver down her spine.

She could still see in her mind's eye the other occupants of the craft as it sped away from a huge cargo ship. There were six men, all of them native islanders, except for a middle-aged Caucasian man whom she did not recognise. He was bound and held captive as well.

The driver had closely cropped black hair, and upon his upper arm was a tattoo of a venomous snake. Another tattoo of a huge ugly spider crawled across the back of his hand. The leader of the group of pirates had worn a bandana and sat on the rim of the zodiac along with his men.

His long black hair had been pulled away from his face by a bandana looped around his forehead and tied at the back. His well-muscled, tattooed chest had shown beneath a shabby black vest that was unbuttoned. Bare feet had protruded from black cotton pants.

One of his comrades had worn a loose sleeveless black shirt without a collar and his trousers had been distinctly military. Across the bridge of his nose and running toward his left ear was a long nasty scar. Both sets of dark eyes had glimmered menacingly. The last villain had been stocky and his eyes were so dark they appeared to be black, almost as black as his soul.

A shudder ran through Charlotte and she was grateful she had awakened from the awful nightmare. She glanced out the dormer window. It was still dark outside, and as yet, there were no orange hues announcing the arrival of dawn.

She was tired but did not want to fall asleep again if it meant returning to that dream. She pulled on one of Lachlan's windcheaters and a pair of his jeans that she had swiped before going to bed. Her own clothes needed a decent wash. The jeans were a little baggy at the waist, but she didn't care. She would borrow a belt from Kade in the morning.

She descended the stairs in bare feet and was surprised to find the lights on. She wandered from the hallway into the open living space and spotted Kade sitting at the table. His elbows rested on the tabletop and his head was bent over a thick book.

Sun bleached curls fell across his forehead as he read. Her heart softened. It was more than his looks that caused the affection stirring in her. There was something just so lovable about him.

And kind. She smiled. *He's really kind.*

She padded quietly to the table and sat opposite him. He glanced at her in surprise.

"What are you doing up?" he asked softly. "Are you feeling alright?"

"Yeah, I'm fine. I had a nightmare."

"I can't sleep either. I keep thinking about Rylie's story."

Charlotte worried her lower lip. "I should probably check on him."

"I already did. He's sleeping peacefully."

Charlotte relaxed. "Thanks." Her eyes dropped curiously to the book on the table. "What are you reading?"

Kade held it up so that she could see the gold lettering on the leather cover. The Holy Bible.

She was intrigued. Spiritual hunger gnawed within her. "What passage are you reading from?"

Kade's right brow quirked subtly. "Psalms. It's soothing."

Desire burned in her light blue eyes. "Read it

aloud?"

Kade appeared slightly amazed and she wondered why. His gaze dropped to the page open before him.

"'God is our refuge and strength, a very present help in trouble. Therefore we will not fear, though the earth be removed, and though the mountains be carried into the midst of the sea; though its waters roar and be troubled, though the mountains shake with its swelling. Selah.'"

Peace settled around Charlotte's heart. Something about those words felt so familiar. It was like coming home. Her mind grasped a hold of them as someone adrift at sea would cling to a rock. Kade read on and she let the words roll over her in a comforting cadence.

"'The Lord of hosts is with us; the God of Jacob is our refuge. Selah. Come, behold the works of the Lord, who has made desolations in the earth. He makes wars cease to the end of the earth; He breaks the bow and cuts the spear in two; He burns the chariot in the fire-'"

"'Be still, and know that I am God'," Charlotte finished for him. She did not know where the words came from, only that they were more familiar to her than her own face was in a mirror. "'I will be exalted among the nations, I will be exalted in the earth! The Lord of hosts is with us; the God of Jacob is our refuge.'"

Kade stared at her in stunned silence. Tears pooled in her eyes and she stared right back.

"Oh Kade," she breathed in wonder, "I know this! Somehow I know this book. When you were reading, I felt as though I had come home."

Kade's face softened with a gentle smile. "Would you like to borrow it for a while?"

She nodded and beamed. "Oh yes!"

He smiled warmly in return and pushed his Bible across the tabletop toward her. She held the book lovingly in her fingers, her eyes caressing its pages. This definitely felt familiar.

Kade watched the tender way she smoothed the thin pages in her hand. Charlotte noted that he did not generally seem given to displays of emotion. But something in the way she had responded to the book he obviously treasured had deeply touched him.

She stood, his Bible still in her hands, and held his pleased gaze. "Thanks Kade."

"You're welcome."

She smiled warmly and wandered toward the stairs and her room, intending to read for as long as she could stay awake.

* * *

Charlotte read until the first rays of dawn peered over the horizon. She began in Luke and read through the entire account of Jesus Christ. She then continued into the book of Acts. She was dazzled by the courage of Jesus' followers and the power God demonstrated through their lives.

Finally she closed Kade's Bible and lay on her back staring at the ceiling that was touched gently by the sunrise out her window. Her heart was full to overflowing.

"God, You amaze me! That You would give up Your precious Son for a world that would scorn and reject Him, is beyond my comprehension. Is the love that compelled You to do that something that You feel for me also?"

She waited in the silence that followed, not really expecting an answer, but hoping there was one out there.

Oh yes, child! Oh yes! The words seemed to materialise in her thoughts from nowhere. They certainly did not belong to her!

Then she sensed it. A comforting presence, powerful, all encompassing, and that seemed to wrap her in Himself. She felt like an eagle tucked safely under the wings of its parent. That was the moment she knew the answer to her question.

She was freefalling into a chasm of love that enveloped her with delight. It was the Father's heart, and the answer was yes.

"Okay, my happy feeling from the clean house has gone," Lachlan remarked the next morning as he observed Charlotte breeze into the room wearing his windcheater and jeans.

Charlotte ignored his annoyed scowl and sent him a cheerful smile. "Good morning, Lachie."

His eyes narrowed. "How can you be so disgustingly happy after what happened last night?"

She sailed through to the kitchen. She made some toast and slid into a chair at the table where Kade was eating breakfast. "Because I discovered last night that God loves me."

Lachlan shook his head from his place at his computer desk and went back to what he was doing.

"You mean re-discovered," Rylie's voice emanated from the hall doorway.

All three heads swivelled his direction. Kade immediately stood and moved toward the injured man leaning against the arch. Rylie waved him aside and forced weak legs to carry him to the sofa. He sank into its soft cushions and rested his head against the couch back.

Kade followed and stared down at him with a look of concern from his place beside the sofa. Charlotte sat beside Rylie. He was doing well to be able to walk around after having lost so much blood the night before.

She noted his extremely pale skin and glazed eyes. "What do you mean 're-discovered'?"

He rolled his head left and met her gaze. "You're a Christian. I introduced you to Jesus four years ago."

"You're a follower of Jesus too?" Kade asked him in astonishment.

Rylie closed his eyes wearily. "Yeah."

"Then how come-" Kade started to ask the obvious question and was swiftly interrupted by Lachlan.

"The hard drive is why he's landed in this mess. Come take a look at this." He continued to click through the files on his screen using a mouse.

"I'll stay here if that's alright with you," Rylie excused himself tiredly and remained on the couch.

Kade and Charlotte wandered to the computer desk and gazed at the screen over Lachlan's shoulder. Charlotte was the first to speak.

"What have you found?"

"If I was the head of ASIO I'd be quaking in my boots right now," Lachlan remarked.

Kade looked a little lost with the jargon. "What's ASIO again?"

"The Australian Security Intelligence Organisation," Charlotte replied without thinking.

Both Lachlan and Kade glanced at her. She shrugged, not knowing where the information had come from. While Kade's eyes lingered on her curiously for a moment, Lachlan focused again on the screen.

"Guys, this is going to blow you out of the water!"

12

"Alright, Tiana, you've been at this all night. Are you going to fill me in?" Detective Sergeant Bodhi Lazzaro asked impatiently around noon.

Tiana was at her desk in the office adjacent to his. He dropped into the chair opposite her and waited. She turned from her screen and folded her hands on the desktop and grinned. "You first."

An amused smile tugged at the corners of his mouth. "Okay. Let's see." He pondered his most recent findings. "A neighbour saw three people climb out of apartment one via the balcony and seconds later a fourth exited through the front door. He fired at a fifth who had taken the handbrake off a black sports car and sent it rolling down the hill.

"The three from the apartment are a bit of a mystery, except that when we traced the call made by Rylie Hunter that evening, it was to a Charlotte Mickleson, who incidentally rents that apartment. The call coincides with the timeframe in which the three exited the apartment and the shooter took out the man who pushed his car down the hill.

"That could mean one of the three intruders was actually Charlotte Mickleson and Rylie made the call." Bodhi watched his partner's face closely and smiled. He could see the pieces coming together in her mind just as his had only moments ago.

"Are you saying that Rylie called Charlotte to warn her someone was coming?"

"I am."

"Why would she enter via the balcony? Why not use a key and go through the front entrance?" Tiana puzzled.

"She might have lost her key."

"I suppose. Okay, this is what I've found," she quickly changed direction. "The blood on the footpath matches the DNA we found at the botanic gardens. It was Rylie Hunter that was shot. The results of the samples we found in the bunker after we followed that tip from Rylie's pastor, Lucas Kennedy, have also come in. It was Rylie's as well."

"So his story checks out," Bodhi mused. "All except for his blood on Hayden Brooker's shirt."

"That could have been planted, just as Rylie claimed when he spoke with Pastor Kennedy," Tiana reasoned.

Bodhi's expression became inquisitive. "I thought you believed he was guilty."

"I go by cold hard evidence, and now the evidence

has tipped in his favour."

Bodhi pondered her statement momentarily and then remembered another crucial piece of information. "As you know, Rylie's best friend is Charlotte Mickleson."

"The one from the apartment."

"Yes. Well, here's the corker." His eyes glimmered with the delight of discovery. "She's one of us."

"A detective?"

"No. She's a probationary constable in the Sydney police force. And get this, she didn't show up for work yesterday or today. I followed Pastor Kennedy's information and contacted the police who rescued the mystery woman on the rocks at South Head Saturday morning. I crosschecked the fingerprints they took from her to help establish her identity. They were an exact match for the prints found everywhere at Charlotte Mickleson's apartment. She is the mystery woman."

Tiana smiled like a Cheshire cat and leaned back in her chair. "So Rylie's story checks out again. Someone pushed her over the cliffs at South Head and took him to the bunker where he later escaped. It seems Rylie found her before we did."

Bodhi's face darkened. "And so did their attacker."

They sat in silence for several thoughtful minutes. Finally Tiana spoke what was on her mind.

"I would love to get my hands on that hard drive, if it truly exists."

"Oh don't you worry, if it exists we'll find it."

Tiana's expression was grim. "Yeah, but so might the shooter."

* * *

"So how do all of these files interrelate?" Charlotte asked the question that had evidently been puzzling Rylie for days.

Both she and Kade had drawn up chairs and were sitting on either side of Lachlan as he waded through the files on the external hard drive. Rylie was fast asleep on the couch in the same position he had occupied for over an hour.

Lachlan and Kade had phoned their respective workplaces and taken several days leave when it became apparent they were now embroiled in a mess of gigantic proportions.

"I'm not sure, but it worries me. You see this bank record? In the past two months it has received significant contributions. The last one was completed the day Rylie's friend Hayden died. It was in the amount of one-hundred thousand dollars. Whoever owns this account is being paid for something and it's my guess that it's shady. I wish I could trace its source."

"The police could," Kade pointed out. "Maybe you should make a copy of everything on that hard drive and give it to them?"

"I plan to," Lachlan replied and went straight back to expounding on the hard drive's contents. "There are three scanned copies of enrolment documents at Sydney University. I can't figure out why they're there but it must be something to do with who these people are."

"Maybe that should be our first port of call?" Charlotte suggested.

"You can do your thing on the computer and find out who they are and why they're so important," Kade put in.

"Already on it."

Charlotte's brow furrowed in thought. "And what about the other files?"

Lachlan glanced down the folders listed on his screen. "E-mails and recorded chat sessions between two to three people. Unfortunately I don't know who they are because they're using pseudonyms. I might be able to find out if I trace their e-mail addresses and hack into the service provider's database. I'll try that in a minute. But check out the stuff they're talking about. It scares me to death." Lachlan clicked into an e-mail and brought it up on the screen for his cohorts to read.

'Avenger says it is in fifteen days. We will meet in the usual place to finalise preparations. He will make contact just prior to the day of vengeance with final instructions.'

"The others are like it. They discuss hatred for America and other western nations. Sometimes they talk about the immorality of our culture, but most of the time they chew over politics. The one you just read was sent five days ago."

"The day before Hayden was killed," Charlotte noted pensively.

"The 'day of vengeance'?" Kade screwed up his face. "That's a little freaky. What's happening in fifteen days?"

"That's what scares me," Lachlan admitted. "It's now ten days. Then there's this mobile phone record. It's a list of numbers one person has called. Some of these numbers are international."

Charlotte's gaze shifted from the screen to Lachlan's face. "Who is the caller?"

"I don't know, but I intend to find out. I'm planning on looking that up and then tracing his location by the GPS in his cell phone. Whoever he is, we'll find out where he lives, where he goes to work, and what he does in his free time."

"Do that now and we'll get onto this guy fast," Kade urged.

"Yeah, but first make a copy of the hard drive. Kade and I can pass it on to the police."

Lachlan did not look pleased about this. "Do it anonymously. You don't want them connecting us with Rylie or we'll all be in trouble."

Charlotte smiled. "I'm glad we've got you on our side, Lachie."

"Yeah well," he remarked in a blasé tone, "at least now we know it's the right side."

Kade rolled his eyes. "We knew that from the beginning."

"Whatever you reckon." Lachlan foraged distractedly in his desk for something large enough to copy the files to. He paused when another possibility entered his mind.

He fetched a pair of gloves from under the kitchen sink and then came back to his desk and opened a brand new package of blank DVDs. It would not do to have his fingerprints on the discs he was anonymously passing on to the police.

"Hey, check this out," Bodhi baited his partner as he strode past her office into his own.

Tiana set aside the ballistics report from the shooting in Manly and followed her partner into his office. He closed the door behind her. Her brows drew together inquisitively. If he wanted privacy then he must have discovered something interesting at the hospital where Charlotte Mickleson had been admitted.

Bodhi dropped his car keys onto his desk and sat his satchel beside them. Tiana continued to watch him curiously, becoming a little impatient when instead of explaining, he dug around in his bag.

"Well? What did you find?"

Bodhi stopped foraging and met her gaze. "Late Saturday afternoon someone showed up at the hospital claiming the woman found on the rocks was his sister."

Tiana's mind began to race. "Charlotte Mickleson's employment records show she is an only child. Was it Rylie or was it our shooter? Did you get a description?"

Bodhi grinned. "I'll go you one better." He pulled a disc from his satchel and waggled his brows.

Tiana's eyes brightened. "You got surveillance footage?"

Bodhi beamed proudly like a boy who had just won a running contest. "Yep."

"Quit grinning like a kid and let's take a look!" she scolded mildly and reached for the disc.

He held it high above her head. "Tsk, tsk, my young

colleague. You must learn the art of patience."

Tiana suppressed a smile and moved to the television in a cabinet in the corner. She turned it on while Bodhi inserted the disc into the DVD player below it. She stood back while he skipped to the time the receptionist said the visitor had made his appearance.

He froze the frame when a man of medium height wearing trendy faded jeans and a black hooded jumper, walked to the reception desk. He was wearing a black baseball cap which concealed the colour of his hair and his facial features. Bodhi pressed play again and they watched as the man conversed with the receptionist with his back to the surveillance camera. He exited shortly after.

Tiana felt some annoyance.

Bodhi skipped back to the visitor's entrance again and echoed her sentiments. "This guy is good. He knows there's a surveillance camera and he keeps his face averted the whole time."

"Yes, but note his height. He's only about five foot seven or five foot eight. Rylie Hunter is over six feet tall. Bodhi, I think we're looking at Charlotte and Rylie's attacker and potentially Hayden Brooker's killer."

Bodhi studied the cagey man on the screen, his keen eyes missing nothing. "You know, for a rookie you're pretty good at detective work."

"Thanks for the compliment." She gave a sarcastic smile and strode for the door.

She had to finish going over the ballistics report. With any luck, the shooter may have left a fingerprint or at least a partial print on the empty bullet cartridge found at the scene.

13

"Lachie, we're getting nothing here," Kade informed his housemate over his cell phone. He had it on speaker so that Charlotte was able to join the conversation. "So far the guy has attended two lectures. Both were sonorously boring by the way."

"Sonorous?" Lachlan snorted in amusement on the other end of the line. "I didn't think you knew any big words."

Kade's look was longsuffering. "Whatever."

He and Charlotte were at Sydney University in the beautiful grounds dotted with ancient shade trees, all of which were dwarfed by the spires and peaked rooftops of the classical sandstone buildings nearby. The university was an architect's delight. It was over one hundred years old and sprawled along Parramatta Road.

It was also crawling with staff and students alike. Thankfully Lachlan had been able to track the caller through the GPS in his mobile to within three metres of his location.

Charlotte and Kade had spent the day trailing the

guy. He was rather short, had brown eyes, black hair and had dark tanned skin, possibly of Middle Eastern heritage. He blended in with Sydney's multinational students, wearing jeans and a t-shirt just like everybody else and speaking English, although with a heavy accent.

"Now he's sitting down to lunch by himself." They were wasting their time!

Charlotte snatched the cell phone from Kade. "One lecturer referred to him as Fahim when he asked a question. Does that help?"

They could hear computer keys on the other end of the line. Lachlan must be drawing information from the hard drive.

"Yeah, it does."

"Why did Hayden focus his search on Fahim?" Rylie's voice came over the connection.

Lachlan must also have his phone on speaker and Rylie had to be sitting with him at the desk.

"I'm acquainted with him. He's polite and rather harmless."

"Well? Come on," Charlotte demanded impatiently.

"Do you remember those enrolment forms on the hard drive I showed you? Fahim Gabir is one of the three students," Lachlan explained.

"Why is Fahim so important that someone would try to kill Rylie and me over his enrolment form and his phone records on a hard drive?"

She and Kade were sitting under a large oak looking like just another couple enjoying a lunch break.

"Give us a minute."

Charlotte could hear computer keys tapping again on the other end of the line.

"How is it you got all upset when you thought you were aiding and abetting a criminal last night, and yet you'll hack into an e-mail service provider to find out someone's identity without a qualm?" Rylie's bemused voice challenged.

"This is different," Lachlan answered reasonably, sounding as though he thought the logic was obvious to the world.

"Hacking is just as illegal as hiding the prime suspect of a crime. It's like checking to see if someone's front door is locked and if it is, breaking in and taking a look around. Then you leave a note that says, 'Hi. You should probably change your locks and tighten up your security.'"

"It's not wrong if the computer you're hacking into is used by a criminal," Lachlan rationalised.

Kade and Charlotte exchanged amused smiles. Rylie had a good point.

"You sound like Hayden," he muttered.

"Yeah, but I'll bet you learned all of his tricks."

"A good portion of which I don't use because my

conscience won't allow me."

"Ah-hah!" Lachlan exclaimed triumphantly. "Kade, Chaz, you're gunna love this!"

"Chaz?" Charlotte raised an eyebrow.

"It's your new nickname," Lachlan informed her matter-of-factly.

Charlotte rolled her eyes and parroted Kade and Lachlan's favourite phrase. "Whatever!"

"Get this! The e-mailer who refers to 'Avenger' is Fahim Gabir. What's the bet the two he e-mailed that note to are the ones from the enrolment forms on the hard drive?"

Now Kade was intrigued. The day of vengeance. Could Fahim actually be involved in terrorist activities? If so, then who was Avenger? He marvelled at Rylie's friend's find. How had he come across all of this and what if it truly was a terrorist attack?

Whatever it was, they had ten days to go and the clock was ticking.

"Yep, I was right. The two guys Fahim e-mails regularly are the same ones on the other enrolment forms. But check this out, all three are from the Middle East. Fahim is from Iraq and the other two are on student visas from Afghanistan."

Kade raised his brows.

"I guess that explains the international calls he made," Charlotte commented.

"Yeah, and I'd like to find out who he's been talking to," Lachlan replied suspiciously.

"I'll get onto that," Rylie offered. "I'll use that print-out of Fahim's phone record from this morning."

"Where are you going?" They heard Lachlan's puzzled tone. "Just call the numbers from here."

Rylie's now distant voice was sceptical. "Are you mad? What if these people are dodgy and the call is being traced? Do you really want questionable people knocking on your door?"

"I hadn't thought of that. Okay."

"Guys, we'll talk to you soon. Let us know how the search goes," Kade concluded the conversation.

"Will do." Lachlan sounded distracted and computer keys hammered consistently in the background.

Kade shook his head and disconnected the line.

"Hey Bodhi." Tiana studied the large, padded envelope in her hands and wandered absently into his office late that afternoon.

He glanced up from the report he was writing. "What is it?"

Tiana dropped into the chair on the opposite side of his desk and tore the envelope open. It was in a padded envelope that simply said, *To the cops on Rylie*

Hunter's case'.

"This was somehow planted in a police vehicle in central Sydney this morning. They brought it over personally just now." She removed several discs from the package. Taped to the top disc was a message.

'You've got him all wrong. Here are the hard drive files that got Hayden Brooker killed and Rylie Hunter framed. Enjoy.'

Tiana smiled in amusement. Someone either had a great sense of humour, or this was the treasure trove she had been chasing.

Hang on, how could anyone know about the hard drive? That was privileged information from Lucas Kennedy. Had Rylie's pastor gone to the media? Not likely. Even if he had, a response from a member of the public this quickly was improbable.

A prankster would not be so meticulous as to leave no fingerprints, and according to the officer who had delivered the discs to the detective branch of the Sydney Police only moments ago, both the envelope and the discs were print free. A thrill of excitement chased through her and she sprang to her feet.

Bodhi frowned in puzzlement and followed her as she hurried to her office. She inserted the top disc into her computer. He picked up the empty package from her desktop and read the note. His interest peaked. He drew up a chair beside her and focused

on the files she was scanning for viruses. Receiving
the all clear from her system's anti-virus, she opened
the disc and began to read.

"Why am I tailing this kid? Do you want me to
do him or what?" Abe questioned irritably from his
place under a jacaranda in the university grounds.

He was on his cell phone to his boss, a man he had
never actually seen, but who paid well. That was all
he needed to know.

"Leave the kid. Look, sooner or later they'll piece
together the files Brooker stole and it'll lead to him.
He's the bait. Hunter and the girl are the fish. When
they show up, and it's only a matter of time until they
do, eliminate them."

"Then do I get to do the kid?"

"No. Killing the kid would nullify the deal and our
money supply would end," his boss returned hotly.
"Stick to the plan and only eradicate who I say. Have
you got that?"

Abe's answer was an abrupt disconnection and a
dial tone in his boss's ear. He pocketed his mobile
and glared at the young man fifty or so metres away,
under a tree eating his lunch outside the university.

He didn't understand why the external hard drive

files were important, or why he had to kill some people and not others. But in the end that did not matter. All he cared about was the money, and frankly, he was raking in enough of that to make it all worthwhile. Nevertheless, frustration and boredom were getting to him.

He scanned the crowd eating on the lawn one more time and something in his mind flicked an adrenaline switch. His eyes swung back for a second look and narrowed dangerously on the tall brunette with light blue eyes sitting casually under an oak beside a man with curly sun bleached hair. His boss had been correct. He smiled with sadistic pleasure.

"Time to go fishing."

14

"Bodhi."

Tiana's senior partner was sitting beside her, eyes intent on her computer screen. They had been working solid for hours sorting through the information on each of the discs and following through on each lead.

The phone and bank records, the photos, the enrolment forms, the seemingly random documents, the e-mails, the encrypted files; they all pointed to something far bigger than they had anticipated.

Tiana was fast concluding that it was no wonder Hayden Brooker was dead and it was only a matter of time before Rylie Hunter was as well. She was starting to feel a little uncomfortable herself.

"Yes?" he answered distractedly.

"Does Rylie Hunter have any idea of the magnitude of what he has stumbled upon?"

Bodhi tore his eyes away from the screen and looked at her gravely. "Probably not. Make some copies of those discs immediately." He picked up the telephone on her desk and punched in a lengthy number.

"Who are you calling?" She glanced at him curiously and began copying files across to her own computer. She would transfer them to her portable hard drive next. It was the only device large enough to store that amount of information.

"ASIO."

Tiana was about to ask him another question when someone on the other end of the line picked up.

"This is Detective Sergeant Bodhi Lazzaro from the Sydney Homicide Squad. May I speak with someone regarding a possible terrorist threat? ... Yes, I'll hold." He covered the receiver with his hand. "Find the name of that bank account holder and see if you can trace the source of those large payments."

"I will. Just let me copy these files first," she insisted with some impatience. No one, despite their gender, was that good at multitasking.

"And find out who Avenger is. Oh, and get the detective inspector in here."

Tiana rolled her eyes. "Would you like me to stand on my head while I'm at it?"

Bodhi reined in a smile. "If you can." His attention quickly diverted.

"Mr. Kitson, it's Detective Sergeant Lazzaro. You need to come to my office as soon as possible. This is something that should be dealt with in person. We've come into possession of some rather disturbing information that requires the immediate attention of your organisation."

* * *

Kade's eyes lingered on Charlotte as she boarded the bus ahead of him. Lachlan's jeans had looked comical on her and so they had stopped to buy some clothes before beginning their surveillance of Fahim that morning. He was still quite taken with how she looked in fresh denim jeans and a white singlet beneath a sheer, violet fitted top with fluted sleeves. She was round in all of the right places and those long legs...

He shook his head. He almost wished she had stayed in Lachlan's oversized pants and roomy windcheater. It would have been easier to concentrate on their mission if she weren't so downright gorgeous. And those eyes! The soft violet of her top only served to accentuate their colour.

News of her faith and rediscovered love for Jesus only made her twice as appealing. He reminded himself of the conversation he had overheard the previous evening and that she was spoken for by Rylie. However, his heart failed to take any notice of the warning.

Kade stepped onto the bus and sat down beside her in a seat toward the back. She smiled, completely oblivious to the effect she was having on him. He returned it half heartedly, forcing himself to focus on the situation at hand.

"What next? Staking out Fahim turned up nothing today."

It was drawing close to six pm and they were both hungry and tired. Thanks to daylight savings, the sun was not due to set for another three hours.

"We go home and see what the boys have found." She bit her lower lip and her brow puckered in curiosity. "Kade?"

"Yeah?" He allowed his gaze to linger on her face. After all, she was talking to him and he had a legitimate excuse to stare.

"What do you do for a living?"

He studied the straight ridge of her elegant nose, the wide innocence of her eyes, the fullness of her mouth. Suddenly she was frowning.

"Kade?"

He snapped out of it. "Yeah?"

"You haven't answered my question." She appeared to be puzzling over his obvious withdrawal. He hoped she assumed it was because of the mess that had landed in his lap.

Kade gave himself a stern mental lecture and then forced himself to concentrate on what she was saying. "What question was that?"

"I was just wondering what you do for a living?"

A cheeky sparkle entered his warm brown eyes. "I'm a checkout chick at Woolworths."

"Kade, guys aren't checkout chicks."

"Then what are they?" he bantered playfully.

"I don't know, they're-" Her eyes took on a suspicious glint. "You're not a checkout worker."

His eyes twinkled mischievously. "What makes you say that?"

"Your eyes. They're full of that sparkle you get when you're pulling my leg."

A smile that revealed straight white teeth appeared and the mischief vanished. "I'm a pilot. I think I already mentioned it once."

Charlotte's eyes widened in surprise. "What do you fly?"

"I work for a commercial business that flies tourists over the harbour in a chopper."

She looked stunned. "You fly helicopters?"

"You seem surprised." His telltale twinkle returned to his gaze.

"I guess you always come across as kind of... I don't know." Charlotte struggled to articulate an impression she had somehow gained.

"A dumb blond?" he chipped in. "Dim-witted? Slow on the uptake? Dense?"

She glared at him. "Now you're teasing me."

"You walked right into it, Chaz." He liked the sound of Lachlan's new nickname for her.

She could not resist a smile. "I don't think you're dim-witted or dense. You're just very disorganised and laidback. I guess I couldn't imagine you having such a serious job."

"You mean a job that requires intelligence." He went straight to the heart of the matter, suddenly serious.

Charlotte became annoyed. "That is *not* what I said and it was not what I was thinking!" Her angry eyes gave him a severe chastening.

His face suddenly broke into a cheeky grin. "Wow, I've never seen you mad. I wondered what it would take."

Her eyes narrowed dangerously. "Kade Haynes, you're-"

"A loveable rogue?"

"That's not what I was going to say!"

If that fire in her eyes was real, he supposed he would be singed around the edges by now. Time to turn on the charm. "Your eyes look even bluer when you're angry."

"I'll show you blue," she threatened, although her ire was cooling quickly under the warmth of his gaze. "Just one little wack and it'll be the colour of the bruise I put on that-" She froze.

He looked at her bemused. "That what?"

She turned a lovely shade of pink and he grinned cheekily. "You're blushing. Whatever you were about to say must have been good."

She poked him in the ribs. He shifted sideways and exclaimed.

"Ow!"

"Stop it, Kade."

"Stop what?" he asked with wide innocent eyes.

"Stop teasing me." She tried to spear him with a glare, but an insubordinate smile tugged at her lips and caused them to twitch.

Kade had all he could do not to kiss her in that moment. Instead he turned his head to look out the window on the opposite side of the bus.

Houses and shops lining the street had turned into skyscrapers, congested traffic and a host of pedestrians on the sidewalk. They were entering central Sydney.

"I'll try, but my word, it's going to be tough! You're an easy mark."

She suppressed another smile and poked him hard in the ribs again. He jumped and brought his hands up in self-defence. He chuckled and watched her distrustfully. From the look on her face, he knew she would probably do it again.

If only he could erase the rascally gleam in his eyes,

then she would leave him alone. But he might as well tell the sun to stand still. It wasn't going to happen. She was too delightful to tease.

The bus came to a stop outside the station at Circular Quay and the doors opened. With one last wary glance at Charlotte, he preceded her. At least seven other people disembarked, adding to the chaotic rush of tourists and native city dwellers traversing the busy Sydney streets.

Once on the sidewalk Kade paused, debating what to do. Have dinner out, or take something home? It was not likely the boys had cooked.

Charlotte glanced at Kade curiously and was about to ask what was wrong when a dark sports car pulled into a parking spot just beyond the train station. It was opposite the city library with its classic structure and large clock tower. She recognised the car. Dread churned in her stomach and her heart rate accelerated.

A man of medium height unfolded from behind the steering wheel. He wore a grey baseball cap, beige cargo trousers and a white t-shirt emblazoned with a design. Standing roughly one-hundred metres away, he turned and across the distance their eyes locked.

Charlotte could feel the chill in his gaze and see a smirk lift the corners of his mouth.

It was him.

15

Charlotte broke eye contact and grabbed Kade by the arm, dragging him into the crowded covered walkway of the train station building. Straight ahead were the waters of Circular Quay. To the left was the train station entrance where people filed through waist high mechanical entries like sheep through a gateway.

Kade caught the panicked expression on her face and anxiety seemed to kick him hard. "What's wrong?" He jogged to keep up with her frantic pace.

She glanced nervously behind. "He's here, Kade."

"Who's here?"

"Who do you think? The bloke that tried to gun Rylie down last night!" she hissed with another look over her shoulder.

The man rounded the corner just as they merged with the crowd of tourists and locals on the walkway by the water's edge. Kade glanced behind and must have spotted the figure now jogging toward them.

He grabbed Charlotte by the wrist and broke into a run, dashing to the right of the station walkway. They dodged in and around people watching the local entertainment.

A band of five aboriginal musicians, three of which were in native attire with painted designs on their bodies, were dancing to rhythmic music for a crowd of tourists. The fourth was playing a didgeridoo and the fifth a small bongo.

Behind them a green, two-storey ferry with yellow siding was leaving, as another just like it was coming in to dock. The Sydney harbour bridge loomed to their left, enormous, grey and imposing. Across the harbour waters skyscrapers and waterfront villas graced the shoreline. To their right, extending slightly out into the harbour was the Sydney Opera House, famous for its six white tiled crescents that made the roof. They seemed to be at odds with one another, four facing the harbour and two facing the city.

Any other day Charlotte would have admired the unusual structure. Today she worked to keep up with Kade and avoid flattening the people they were charging past.

He bent over slightly so as not to be so visible, weaving slowly now through the crowd. Charlotte copied his movements. She was relatively tall, but Kade was even easier to spot in the crowd with his height and curly blond hair. The crowd was thinning, which meant that their cover was as well. Kade stopped and chanced a peek above the crowd. Charlotte did the same.

A familiar figure wearing a grey baseball cap jumped to see above the heads of those milling around him. He repeated the action and then stood still, assessing the situation.

"We're going to double back and try to get to that ferry docking." Kade nodded to the green boat now nudging the covered-in floating platform.

"But won't he be expecting that? I mean, there's no other way out of here but by ferry." Charlotte followed Kade back through the crowd, walking closer to the water.

The grey hat continued to walk toward the opera house, bobbing in amongst the crowd. Beneath its brim she could just imagine those cold, penetrating eyes scanning the sea of faces. Abruptly the hat stopped and turned around.

Charlotte and Kade continued to slide casually through the crowd toward the ticket booth at the entrance of the covered floating platform. Nearby a man dressed in a Captain Cook costume tipped his navy 1700's style hat at Charlotte and then posed for a photograph with a young boy and his mother.

They rounded the ticket booth and stopped. Charlotte peered around the corner and spotted the grey cap pushing through the crowd. She drew her head in moments before his face became visible.

"He's doubled back and is coming right toward us."

Kade glanced around, his mind clearly scrambling for another route of escape. The ferry was not going to work. "He's banking on us needing to take either the ferry or a train. He figures we would have turned back sooner or later and he's going to watch the station entrance and the dock like a hawk until we do."

"This isn't good." Charlotte frantically searched for another way out.

"I've got an idea." Kade tugged her onto the walkway heading toward the harbour bridge.

Charlotte glanced over her shoulder and spotted him twenty metres behind. He turned in a circle, methodically inspecting each face in his vicinity. His eyes locked with hers. She did not wait to see his response, but pulled Kade into a run.

"He saw me!" She cast one more glance over her shoulder.

Sure enough, he was barging through the crowd in hot pursuit. A woman pushing a pram was shoved aside. The pram landed on its side on the pavement and the woman let out a shriek. Passersby exclaimed, asked questions and pointed at the retreating back of the man charging through the crowded walkway like a bull in a china shop.

Kade led them to the left past a large raised circular Sydney Cove 1808 map in the pavement. He then took them by the garden beds and under the railway tracks a storey above them, onto the same street where they had disembarked from the bus.

He sprinted across an intersection onto the street running away from Circular Quay, overshadowed by tall skyscrapers on each side. A car jammed on its brakes and skidded, barely missing Charlotte as she followed in his wake.

They reached the sidewalk and ran headlong into the crowd of people coming and going after their day at work. A glance behind them confirmed that they had not lost the guy.

"What do we do now?" Charlotte saw the man dodging traffic to get to them.

Kade dug his cell phone from his pocket. "I'm calling in a favour." He dialled as they jogged. "Just pray it works?"

"Oh I'm praying already! Who are you calling?"

"A friend."

They reached the corner just as the person on the other end of the line answered. Kade turned left and they continued to run.

"Where are we going?" Charlotte was breathing hard. She looked behind them.

The gunman rounded the corner as well. Kade did not answer.

"Jack, it's Kade." He wasted no time. "Are you in the air?"

Charlotte listened to half of the conversation as they ran, wondering what on earth he was up to.

"I know you took my shift. I don't have time to talk. Are you in the air? ... Good. Where are you? ... Look mate, this is life and death. I need a big favour and I need it right now.

"This is going to sound crazy but you have to do what I say and don't ask any questions. I want you to land in the botanic gardens out the front of parliament house. ... No! Not in the grounds you doof! On the grass outside the fence! ... I said don't ask any questions. I've got a madman chasing me with a gun and he tried to kill us last night. If you don't come I'm a dead man! Just do it!" He disconnected the line and darted left at the end of the street.

Charlotte recognised the Opera House ahead of them. They had basically run around the block and were now headed through a walkway that led straight to it. Only instead of continuing, Kade made a sharp right onto Macquarie Street, which was adjacent to the Opera House and the botanic gardens.

Charlotte ran across the road after him, narrowly missing a bus. They sprinted up a grassy hill, on top of which were various deliberately strewn chunks of carved stone, taken from historic buildings and bridges that had been demolished in the last century.

They reached the top of the hill and headed down the other side onto a footpath. Charlotte's lungs burned and her head pounded.

Hang on a moment! That was not her head pounding. It was the sound of rotor blades beating the cool spring air. A huge colony of startled fruit bats lifted from the trees of the botanic gardens ahead and winged their way toward the city.

Suddenly Kade stumbled and fell, accompanied by a surprised exclamation and a terrible thud when his skin met the pavement. Charlotte, only two paces behind him, pulled him to his feet. He staggered and then regained his balance.

Together they rounded the corner and charged down into an open grassy field surrounded by a wide variety of trees. In the centre, a black helicopter lowered slowly from the sky one-hundred metres away. They ran straight for it.

Something bit at Charlotte's left arm and she clutched it in bewilderment. A quick look told her it was bleeding. With a glance over her shoulder understanding was swift in its arrival.

Standing with feet apart roughly fifty metres behind them, an arm raised and pointing their way, was the gunman. He aimed and fired the weapon in his hand.

Charlotte darted right, grabbing Kade's arm as he ran beside her. She shoved him. Something hissed past her left ear.

She shouted to be heard above the roar of the helicopter setting down twenty metres away. "He's shooting at us! It's hard to hit a moving target, so keep dodging!" She darted right.

Adrenalin fuelled his steps and Kade dodged with her. Another shot ripped into the grass near their feet. Only five metres to go. Like angry wasps, three more shots whizzed past them, barely missing the ducking, weaving targets.

Charlotte dropped and rolled under the front of the helicopter and came up on the other side. She wrenched open the passenger door and climbed in, with Kade hot on her heels. He pulled the door shut behind them.

"What in the blazes is-" The pilot's astounded cry was cut short by a bullet ploughing into the passenger window.

Charlotte and Kade hit the floor, along with two terrified European tourists who began screaming and shouting in what sounded like German.

"Take off! Take off!" Kade commanded the pilot, who seemed to be in a stunned stupor.

Another bullet penetrated the helicopter, this time only inches from the pilot's head. With an exclamation of both surprise and terror, he powered up the chopper and it lifted into the air. He veered it toward the harbour, just skimming the trees on the edge of the botanic gardens in his bid for escape.

Charlotte managed a glimpse out the passenger window. The shooter was fleeing the park, along with several startled people who had previously been enjoying its serenity.

She breathed a sigh of relief and sat up. The German couple, a middle-aged man and presumably his wife, were still on their knees on the floor with their hands over their heads. Kade sat up and blinked. He looked as though he was feeling light-headed.

"Thanks Jack," he said with a grateful sigh. "We owe you."

"What was that about?" his colleague demanded as he took the chopper out over the water.

Charlotte noticed him cringe. "Are you alright?"

"Yeah, it's just that fall I took. I felt like I got hit by a sharp rock." He reached up to touch the tender area a few inches from his forehead and Charlotte's eyes followed his hand's progress.

Her eyes widened in horror. "Kade, you've been shot!"

16

"I can't find anything on Avenger," Tiana admitted to Bodhi when he checked in with her a few hours later. "Whoever he is, he's left a clean trail. However," she added with a telltale gleam in her intelligent eyes, "the bank account holder who received those generous payments, is Bianca Gillham, a twenty-two year old woman who worked in a petrol station in central Canberra.

"She dressed like a Goth and led a lonely life, no family or close friends. But get this, she was a genius with computers, a hacker."

Bodhi frowned. "Why are you talking about her in the past tense?"

Tiana's face was grim. "She's dead. Her body was found this morning by a hiker along one of the trails on the outskirts of Canberra. Homicide down there say she's been dead for a few days."

Bodhi sighed and dropped into the spare chair in her office. "Okay, let me get this straight. A hacker is paid a generous sum of money and about a week later is found dead. Who paid her for her services and what was it she was asked to hack into?"

"I'm not sure, but Hayden Brooker fits in the picture quite well. He was a nerd too, and for some unknown reason, had a copy of her files. That suggests he used some kind of trojan, worm or even keylogger to hack into her computer and gain access to her information. Now he too is dead. How does that tie in with the possible terrorist threat and how did he know her?"

"It has something to do with what she was being paid for. Whatever it was, Hayden was onto her," Bodhi summed it up.

"And whoever made the payments wanted no witnesses left to tell what that job was."

"She knew too much." Bodhi looked at Tiana pensively. "Are you able to trace who the payment came from?"

Tiana pulled a face. "Tried that. Whoever forked out the money covered their tracks well. It was a cash deposit made by Bianca."

"So she was paid cash in hand." Bodhi stared at the wall behind his partner for several unseeing moments, deep in thought. He slapped his knees and abruptly stood. "Alright, good work."

He was about to leave when a call from a fellow officer summoned him to the front desk. Standing on the other side of the counter in a crisp white shirt and black jacket, with polished black shoes peeking out from beneath black dress trousers, was a man Bodhi guessed to be in his early thirties. He had straight brown hair, a few rakish strands falling across his forehead and drawing attention to blue eyes Bodhi guessed most girls would fall all over themselves for.

He was not overly tall, although muscles from regular exercise at a gym filled out his shirt. He was not someone Bodhi was anxious to mess with in a scuffle. However, an easygoing smile was forthcoming and the man reached across the counter to shake the detective's hand.

"You must be Joedy Kitson from ASIO." Bodhi returned the handshake with a hearty grip.

"I am. What is it you've found?" Gravity doused the amiable light in his eyes.

"Come this way, Mr. Kitson." Bodhi gestured with his hand for the gentleman to precede him past the counter to his office.

Charlotte took Kade's face between her hands and turned him so she could see the wound more clearly. Blood oozed from a long gash in his hairline on the right side of his head. She breathed a sigh of relief. It was superficial.

"A bullet grazed that hard skull of yours. Thankfully it seems to have penetrated nothing more than skin and muscle. You may need a few stitches." She released him. "Take off your t-shirt."

Kade frowned at her in bewilderment and her expression turned dry.

"I need to stop that bleeding and I'm certainly not taking off my shirt."

"Oh." Kade tugged his t-shirt over his head and winced as it brushed the open gash.

The German couple slowly sat up during this exchange and stared in a stupor at the new passengers. Kade delicately touched the t-shirt to his wound, wincing again in discomfort. Charlotte sighed in exasperation and pushed her hand down over his to apply pressure.

"Ow! What are you doing?" he demanded in very real pain.

She kept her hand in place over the wound. "Stopping the bleeding!"

Kade glimpsed something on her arm that was reaching past his face and pulled it away for a better look with his free hand.

"Kade, I know it hurts but you'll just have to-"

He cut her off with a wry observation. "You're bleeding too, in case you haven't noticed."

She removed her left arm from his gentle grip and inspected the graze just above her elbow. She was fuming. "I know. That wretch ruined my brand new top!"

Kade could not resist an amused smile. "Chaz honey, you're lucky the bullet didn't tear your arm to shreds, or worse yet, kill you."

Charlotte's gaze whipped up to meet his. Did he just call her honey? Kade must have realised his slip of the tongue and quickly changed the subject.

"Could you drop us at Watson's Bay please, Jack? And if anyone comes looking for us, call the police straightaway."

Jack's simmering gaze was fixed out the cockpit windshield. He was clearly outraged. "I'm already planning on doing that. Why was that maniac shooting at you?"

"Deadly secrets, that's why," Kade replied grimly and let his gaze drift down to the water rippling far below.

Joedy Kitson's handsome face was wreathed with concern. "Has anyone outside of this department seen what's on these discs?"

He was standing in front of the closed door, ready

to leave with the discs that were packaged and in his left hand. His right was on the door handle. Tiana answered a split second before her partner could.

"No," she lied.

Bodhi observed her poker face.

"And has anyone made any copies of them?" the ASIO officer queried next, this time looking at her.

She did not like the nature of the question and so she lied again. "No. We were too busy sifting through what was on them."

"I'm only asking because it seems that everyone who gets their hands on these has either wound up dead or has come awfully close to it. Has anyone else in the homicide branch, barring you two, been privy to what is on them?"

Bodhi appeared curious at Tiana's caution. True, they were logical questions. She would have asked them herself.

"Just the inspector," he answered calmly, looking like he wanted to have words with his partner as soon as the man left.

"Alright." Joedy nodded, lost momentarily in thought. "I'd appreciate it if you would keep this quiet for awhile? If a terrorist attack is being planned, then we don't want the perpetrators to know we're onto them."

"Makes sense." Bodhi stood. He shook the man's

hand and then the ASIO officer departed.

Bodhi closed the door behind him and turned to face his partner. With a curious glint in his eyes he raised a speculative brow. "You don't trust him."

Tiana held his gaze. "After what we've discovered, I don't trust anyone."

He smiled in mild amusement, yet he did not argue with her logic.

"Wow, that's him alright," Lachlan commented later that evening.

He copied surveillance video taken from the street cameras in central Sydney onto his computer and printed a still image of the gunman.

Kade shook his head in amazement as he leaned over Lachlan's shoulder to better see the screen. "How did you get such great footage of the chase? That photo will nail the guy!"

Lachlan shrugged modestly. "I just hacked into the database and accessed the security footage from the cameras on the streets at the rough time you gave me, and voila! If it was a closed circuit security system I wouldn't be able to do it."

Kade's brows quirked in bewilderment. "I have no idea what you're talking about, but thanks." He picked up the photograph as it emerged from the printer and studied the man who had attempted to take their lives that day.

The street camera had captured his face clearly as he ran across the road, dodging traffic. His malicious gaze was intent upon the crowd just ahead of him, where Kade and Charlotte were pushing between pedestrians.

Kade's expression held determination and alertness while Charlotte's eyes were wide with fear. She was a step behind Kade, her hands in front of her as she squeezed past a woman in a miniskirt and a short, portly fellow in a suit going in the opposite direction. Even now Kade marvelled that they were still alive.

Jack had dropped them off in Watson's bay where they had gone to a small clinic. The gash from the bullet on Kade's head had been stitched closed and the doctor had also cleaned the small graze on Charlotte's arm. He had asked probing questions about how they had received the injuries, to which the couple had remained unanimously tight-lipped.

Now it was close to eight pm and they were home again. Rylie was in the kitchen scrounging up something for them all to eat while the other three studied the footage of the shooter. Lachlan had downloaded shots taken from two different cameras and pieced them together, and then he had burned them to disc to be sent to the police.

Rylie placed a hot casserole dish on the counter. "Dinner's done. Come and get it."

Kade passed the photograph to Charlotte who was standing on the other side of Lachlan. She studied it closely with an absorbed frown, searching for details that may have been overlooked. Finally she sat it next to the mouse and trailed the boys to the kitchen.

They were spooning large amounts of potato bake onto plates when she arrived. When all of their plates were laden with the delicious smelling food, the four of them sat down around the table. Kade gave God thanks and then conversation began rolling.

"Tell them what you found, Rylie," Lachlan encouraged as he spooned cheesy potato into his mouth.

Kade and Charlotte looked at the man in question curiously. Rylie continued to push the food on his plate in small, uninterested circles.

"Fahim's mobile phone record showed that he called predominantly only four people. Two we matched to the e-mails and the enrolment forms, another to his aunt in Iraq and the last a man named Ahmed Rahim, also an Iraqi. He seems to be a family friend.

"What I found interesting, was Ahmed. When I Googled his name, I discovered his brother was one of Saddam Hussein's top generals. He was assassinated after the U.S and allied troops invaded Iraq."

"So he would have motive to hate the western nations," Lachlan observed around a mouthful.

"Yeah, but that doesn't make him a terrorist," Charlotte countered reasonably.

Rylie continued idly pushing his food around his plate. "We know that." He glanced up at his friends. "I think it's time for me to hand myself in."

All three heads spun to look at him in incredulity.

Lachlan was aghast. "But we're getting so close to proving your innocence!"

Charlotte's concerned gaze held Rylie's. "Yeah, it won't be long now."

He dropped his eyes to his plate. His pensive expression said he had thought about this a lot. Kade too had been rather reflective since their close encounter with death in the garden.

It had been good that Rylie had not turned himself in at his pastor's place. Otherwise he would not have been able to warn them and the gunman would have killed them at Charlotte's apartment. However, now they were all homicide cases waiting to happen.

Rylie sighed and pushed his plate aside. "I think it would be the wisest thing to do. At least then you can all be put under police protection. Today's chase won't be the last, I can guarantee it. We'll all be lucky if we get out of this alive."

"Then who will continue investigating?" Lachlan objected.

"Don't be arrogant." Kade's tone was calm, but his words cut deep into Lachlan's pride. "What makes you think we're the only ones who can discover the truth?"

Lachlan's eyes shot sparks across the table at his housemate.

"Kade's right," Charlotte came to his defence. "Now that the police have the files, I'm sure they're coming to the same conclusions we are. In fact, they'll be able to piece it all together a whole lot quicker than us, because they can access information and resources we can't."

Lachlan did not look pleased, although he refrained from argument. It was three to one and he obviously knew he could not win.

17

Rylie was feeling absolutely wrung out. He had spent a night in a police station jail. He had no appetite and therefore had no food intake. He had been grilled for the past hour and now his glazed eyes roamed the interrogation room.

The walls were a soft blue and the only furniture was a wooden table that had scratches and pen marks all over it. There were three matching chairs that had both seen better days.

In the chair opposite Rylie was Sergeant Guthrie and Senior Constable Lorenz. Sergeant Guthrie was a time-weathered character who had to be in his fifties. His grey hair was short and receding around his forehead, and his slate grey eyes were penetrating.

Rylie knew it was not possible that someone could read his mind, but the cool eyes watching him came pretty close. They read every gesture, noted every bead of sweat, and his probing questions were designed to push the suspect to breaking point, and hopefully confession.

Senior Constable Lorenz was a woman with equally

shrewd eyes and an unreadable expression. Rylie could not tell if she believed him, but by this point he no longer cared. He only hoped that his three friends were faring better than he was. They had also been detained for questioning the night before when they had escorted him to the local police station.

"If you didn't kill Hayden Brooker, then explain how your blood was found on his clothing," Sergeant Guthrie demanded in a hard, emotionless voice. "And also explain to us, Mr. Hunter, how over one-hundred illegal copies of the latest movies were found in your apartment, along with numerous others on your personal computer ready for burning. Not to mention the threatening e-mails in Brooker's inbox from you when he found out what you were doing."

Rylie sank down on his seat and let his head fall against the chair back. He was exhausted and felt like his body's internal combustion was about to explode. He could not think clearly and his head was swimming.

Please God, get me out of here? You know I didn't do it. Please help them to see that?

In answer to his prayer, God's calm nestled about his heart and created a buffer zone.

"Mr Hunter!" Senior Constable Lorenz's sharp tone sliced through his clouded awareness. "You haven't answered our questions."

"Yes I have," Rylie replied blandly, "but you refuse to believe me." He knew that his examiners hoped to fluster and provoke him, or at the very least intimidate him. But he was beyond feeling panic, had past frustration, and had left anxiety well and truly behind.

The two officers exchanged glances, their aggravation thinly veiled. They were getting nowhere. Unexpectedly, the one door into the room opened and a young male officer stepped partially inside.

"Excuse me, there is a Detective Sergeant Bodhi Lazzaro here. He wants to speak with the sergeant on watch."

Sergeant Guthrie muttered under his breath in exasperation and rose from his chair. He strode from the room, gesturing for Senior Constable Lorenz to follow him. The door clicked shut behind them and Rylie sighed with relief.

He leaned forward and laid his arms on the table, resting his head on his forearms. His eyes slid shut and he could feel sleep tugging at the edges of his consciousness. He gave in to its pull and let his mind drift blithely. Rational thoughts turned to nonsensical dreams and he allowed them to carry him away.

✳ ✳ ✳

Bodhi stepped into the interview room ahead of Sergeant Guthrie, who closed the door behind them. Getting the dedicated officers at the station to release Rylie Hunter into his custody had been a difficult battle. However, after Tiana's convincing display of digital and forensic evidence in his favour, they had relented. She now waited in the foyer with the young man's three anxious friends.

Bodhi studied the twenty-year-old with his head resting upon his arms atop the table. "Rylie."

He waited for his head to come up. The young man did not move. Was he giving them the silent treatment?

"Mr. Hunter!" Sergeant Guthrie barked. "The detective is talking to you. Have the good manners to at least look the man in the eye considering he is giving you the benefit of the doubt!"

Rylie stirred and focused bleary eyes on the two tall figures looming over him. He blinked and rubbed his weary face. "I must have fallen asleep."

Bodhi frowned in puzzlement and noted the redness in the young man's cheeks and his glazed eyes. He looked ill. "Are you feeling alright?"

Rylie worked slowly to process the simple question. "Not really."

He looked like he wanted to go back to sleep. Bohdi wondered why he wasn't curious about the newcomer, or over Sergeant Zealous' comment that had broken into his sleep. All he seemed capable of was a blank stare.

Bodhi touched the young man's forehead with his hand and silently fumed that no one had noticed the poor kid was burning up with fever. He crouched in front of him, softening his tone.

"Rylie, please look at me."

Rylie obeyed, clearly having to force his sluggish mind to concentrate.

Bodhi quickly put two and two together. "Your friends outside explained what happened. They also said you were shot in the arm. Which one?"

"My left," he managed with a slow owlish blink.

"May I take a look?" Bodhi took the slight nod he received as agreement.

He rolled up the windcheater sleeve and carefully unwound a bandage. Sure enough, there were distinct bullet entry and exit holes surrounded by raw, infected flesh.

Sergeant Guthrie's eyes widened in surprise and he looked as though guilt was now nagging at the back of his mind. Bodhi saw that the other man had mistaken the suspect's heavy perspiration for fear and anxiety, when it had actually been a high temperature.

"This wound is several days old and unfortunately

it's infected. Come on." He stood and sighed in resignation. "Let's get you to a doctor."

"Bodhi, this is crazy and you know it," Tiana remarked that evening as he rolled out the last mattress he had in his house.

"Yeah, my girlfriend already said as much."

He took a spare pillow from the built in wardrobe while Tiana unrolled a sleeping bag. She would be staying with Charlotte in Bodhi's spare room, while Rylie took the couch and Kade and Lachlan slept on the living room floor.

Witness protection had not been offered. This was the only solution he could come up with to keep the four amateur investigators alive. They were all also on edge with the horrifying news of the detective inspector's death in a tragic car accident that afternoon.

Tiana and Bodhi suspected foul play but could not prove it. If his death was related to the hard drive files he had been privy to, then they were next in line for the axe. It was frightening.

However, personally seeing to the safety of the four key witnesses while also possibly being the next targets, was pure madness. And yet here they were, trying to settle them into Bodhi's 1920's style home in Sydney suburbia.

Bodhi strode to the doorway and glanced back at his partner. "Keep your baton handy, Tiana."

Her sober gaze met his. "I will. I've also got my handgun loaded and the safety on. It'll sleep close to me tonight."

Bodhi smiled and shook his head. They were probably just being paranoid. "Goodnight." He went to check if the shower was finally free.

Tiana climbed into track pants and a comfortable t-shirt and crawled beneath the covers of the spare bed. She was beat.

Charlotte gently placed a cool face washer on Rylie's hot brow. He was huddled beneath a blanket on the sofa shivering with cold and simultaneously burning up.

The doctor had properly seen to the gunshot wound in his arm and had prescribed antibiotics for the infection. Nevertheless, he was still battling with fever until his medicine could take effect. He smiled at her appreciatively despite shivering lips.

Kade listened to their conversation as he climbed into a sleeping bag on a mattress on the floor nearby.

"Rylie, I've been having a strange recurring dream lately," she admitted thoughtfully.

His shoulders shuddered as his body worked to overheat the bug in his system, and then to chill it out. "What about?"

"I keep dreaming I'm in a zodiac held hostage with another man by five pirates, and we're speeding toward some tropical island." She sat cross-legged on the floor at the head of the couch. They were eye to eye. "Then I'm walking through thick jungle with you. It's weird."

Rylie smiled as he shivered beneath the rug. "Thank You God!"

She frowned at his odd reaction and he explained with a chuckle.

"Charlie, it's not a dream. It's a memory. That's how we met. Your dad's cargo ship was hijacked and you were both kidnapped by pirates and taken to Gabriel Island, in the Pearl Isle off the Australian coast.

"You fell out of the boat and they thought you'd drowned so they sailed off. You surfaced and swam to the beach. A day later you found and rescued me."

Charlotte looked stunned and a little doubtful. "Rescued you?"

"I was kidnapped by a man named Zacutti, to blackmail my dad's executive into smuggling drugs on one of his cargo ships, which happened to be the one your dad was sailing.

"The pirates got wind of the drugs on board and that's why they hijacked it. You got me away from the shack where Zacutti had me drugged. A few days later we ran into the Australian navy who got us out of there."

Kade was astounded. "That was you? I remember watching that report. It was all over the news for days. It happened four years ago, right?"

Rylie nodded wearily and his eyes drifted shut. Everything Kade was learning about Rylie was a surprise. The man's faith was genuine and his character gentle and kind. He had not uttered a complaint about his circumstances or the physical discomfort he was in.

Instead he put the needs and safety of others ahead of his own, protecting Charlotte, turning himself in, even down to the simple act of cooking for them all the previous night when he had been coming down with a fever.

When his temperature had soared that very afternoon and Bodhi had finally managed to get him home, the delirious words that fell from his lips had been prayers. He was deeply wounded over being hunted and framed, as evidenced by the honest pleas that spilled from his hurting soul.

What astonished Kade was the psalms that he

quoted word for word in his delirious state, songs written by King David in his distress. He hated to admit it, but Rylie Hunter was a good man and very much deserving of Charlotte's love.

Kade did not know how it was possible to fall in love with someone after only a few days, and yet it had happened. Charlotte was something special and he was greatly disappointed that he would have to step aside and forego the privilege of spending his life loving and getting to know her. Rylie already held that position, and from all appearances, he had well and truly earned it.

"Tell me more?" Charlotte asked, as an eager child would ask for another bedtime story.

Rylie forced heavy eyelids open. "What do you want to know?"

"Do I have any family?"

"Yes, and you should call them tomorrow. I don't know why I didn't think of it earlier." His answer was somewhat muffled by the pillow.

Charlotte opened her mouth to voice another question and it died on her lips. His eyelids had drifted shut again and it would only be a matter of minutes before he was sound asleep.

"Goodnight Rylie."

A faint smile touched his lips. "Mmm," he acknowledged wearily.

She watched him silently for several moments before the gentle sound of rustling must have reminded her they were not alone. She rose stiffly and stretched out the kinks in her limbs, while allowing her gaze to drift to Kade.

Charlotte smiled warmly. He returned it, although he could not extinguish the sad light in his usually lively eyes.

"Are you alright?"

He appreciated the concern in her question, but disappointment was riding him hard. "I'm fine."

She raised a curious brow at his crisp tone. "You're a bit snippy. Is your head still sore? I can get you another panadol."

His heart twisted painfully in his chest. He loved it when her caring attentions were directed toward him, which had happened quite a bit over the last twenty-four hours. He gentled his response. "No, I took one not long ago. But thanks for checking."

He held her gaze and they simply drank in the sight of one another. She released him with a smile and a friendly goodnight. He watched her head to the spare room and his heart became prayerful.

God, I don't know what You've got in mind for my future, but wow, I wish it included her!

18

"Rylie!"

The blood-curdling scream awoke the house in the early hours of morning. Tiana sat bolt upright in bed, her baton already in her left hand while her right foraged on the bedside table for her gun.

Adrenaline cleared the last remnants of sleep from her mind as Charlotte let out another terrified scream from the floor beside her. Tiana's hand landed upon cold hard steel.

The bedroom door slammed open against the wall and suddenly the light flicked on. Tiana's right hand came up with her pistol at the same time Bodhi stepped into the room brandishing his own.

His alarmed gaze swept the room for an intruder, finding only Charlotte now sitting upright sobbing and his partner looking dishevelled and aiming her gun at him.

"Don't shoot!" He raised his hands in surrender, eyes wide in alarm.

In that split second of recognition, Tiana exhaled in relief and lowered her weapon. Three other startled figures charged past him, Kade first, Lachlan second and Rylie bringing up the rear.

"What's going on?" Lachlan was the first to speak, his wide eyes assessing the scene.

Kade saw tears streaming down Charlotte's lovely face and thought he could make a pretty good guess what had happened. He crossed the floor and knelt beside her. He gently lifted her chin with a finger and glassy eyes met his worried gaze.

"It's alright, it was just a dream."

Large crocodile tears spilled onto her long lashes, breaking his heart with each drop of moisture. She seemed to finally notice she was not alone, her watery gaze moving from Kade to the other occupants of the room. Her eyes locked with Rylie's and she sighed deeply with relief.

"You're okay." Her voice was shaky and her chin trembled, seeming to possess a will of its own.

Tiana threw herself back against her pillow with an exasperated growl. Bodhi ran a frustrated hand through his dishevelled hair, obviously aware of how close he and Tiana had come to pulling the trigger.

Lachlan wearily rubbed his face, shook his head and shuffled out of the room. Rylie came forward on uncertain legs and sank weak-kneed onto the end of Charlotte's mattress. Her terrified scream had clearly frightened the living daylights out of him, wrenching him from a deep sleep.

Her left hand unconsciously clutched Kade's t-shirt sleeve, however her eyes remained riveted on Rylie. "I dreamt he hit you and you didn't get up. Then he-" She swallowed a sob.

Kade raised a knowing eyebrow and glanced at Rylie, who managed only a stunned blink. Bodhi frowned in puzzlement and sat his handgun on the tallboy dressing table just inside the door.

"It sounds to me like it was another memory." Kade stroked her back in gentle circles. She did not seem to notice the touch, although her breathing calmed considerably and she stopped crying.

Tiana rolled onto her side and propped herself up on an elbow. "More like it was her mind piecing together what she's been told."

"Not necessarily," Kade reasoned.

"Tell us about the dream from start to finish," Rylie requested in a soft voice, his body beginning to shake all over again.

Bodhi leaned against the tallboy and smothered a yawn.

"I dreamt Rylie and I got off the ferry at Watson's Bay. We were talking about the provisions we were going to buy the next day, because we were going whale watching in his parents' boat that weekend. We bought fish and chips at Doyle's and we sat down at a park bench to eat.

"Rylie was exclaiming over a huge fried prawn he was about to eat and held it up for me to see. A seagull swooped over his head and snatched it from his hand. It landed nearby and gobbled it up and I laughed.

"We finished eating and went for a walk while we waited for the next ferry to Manly. We ended up at the top of the cliffs where we watched the sun set. It was dark when suddenly someone clubbed Rylie from behind and he fell. I screamed his name but he didn't get up.

"A split second later the guy grabbed me and hit me on the side of the head. I crumpled to the ground and saw him crouch beside Rylie. I tried to get up but I couldn't, so I called him again. He didn't answer.

"I took my mobile phone from my pocket and started to key in triple zero. Then the attacker kicked it from my hand. He asked me something about a hard drive but I didn't know what he was talking about and all I could think of was Rylie.

"I called his name again, but my speech was slurred. The man grabbed me by the arms and pulled me to my feet. My knees buckled and I couldn't stand, but it didn't matter. He was strong.

"He lifted me over the safety railing and gave me a shove. I felt myself falling." Charlotte gulped down the terror rising in her throat and finished relaying the awful dream.

"I hit the water hard and before I could even surface, a huge wave dumped me onto a rock. I crawled away from the water and then it all went dark. That's when I woke up."

Kade wrapped his arms around her from side on and she clung to him and wept. Rylie's expression, although compassionate, held a great deal of relief.

"It sounds to me like her mind has played with the details you all shared," Tiana reiterated her earlier opinion.

Tears of sadness for Charlotte and also relief for himself clouded Rylie's vision. "No, it was definitely a memory. I never told her about the seagull stealing my prawn, and it all happened exactly as she said."

A slow smile stole across Bodhi's face and he rubbed the dark stubble on his chin. "Well I'll be," he muttered. "We've finally got our witness and you've got an alibi."

Tiana rubbed her strained eyes the next day at

work and leaned back in her desk chair. She had been tinkering with the encrypted files on the discs for over two hours now, while Bodhi chased up more leads.

Rylie was slouched in a chair opposite her desk swathed in a throw rug off Bodhi's couch. The worst of his fever had abated with the antibiotics and paracetamol in his system. He watched her with curiosity. "What are you doing?"

She sighed and her fingers went back to the keys of her computer. She answered as she worked. "I'm trying to break the encryption on some of these files."

Rylie looked bored and ready for a challenge. "Mind if I try?"

She stopped and levelled him with a sceptical stare. "You?"

He shrugged. "Why not?"

With a doubtful smile, she stepped away from her computer and gestured with a sweep of her hand for him to be seated in her chair. A gleam of eager challenge entered his eyes and he suppressed a smile tugging at the corners of his mouth.

He sat in her swivel chair and shimmied it closer to the desk, frowning when his knees would not fit beneath it. He glanced at her standing beside him, his eyes running from her face to her toes. He shook his head and lowered the chair with tweak of a lever.

Tiana could not resist an amused smile.

"I know, you don't have to say it. I'm short."

Rylie grinned and focused on the screen before him. He began tapping away at the keys, and for a while Tiana watched him work. She eventually shook her head at his failed attempts to crack the encryption and strolled from her office to get a coffee.

Rylie worked steadily while she was gone, using as many of Hayden's tricks as he could remember. He was down to the last two when Tiana wandered back into the office with a steaming mug cradled in her hands.

She dropped into the chair he had been occupying for the past hour and sipped her drink. She studied him for a moment and lifted the mug to her lips for another robust mouthful when a triumphant "Yes!" froze its progress.

Rylie grinned at her over the monitor. "We're in."

Her jaw dropped incredulously. "You're kidding! You can't have broken the encryption that quickly. Not after I've spent the last two hours working on it!"

But Rylie wasn't listening. His brows knit in concentration as he scanned the contents of the files, which were now in a readable format.

"Hey, you should come take a look at this."
Tiana was out of her chair in a heartbeat.

19

Tiana was stunned. "I don't understand, Mr. Teague. How can you not know about these files? They're from your department." She could hear computer keys on the other end of the line.

"I'm sorry, but we have no record of ever investigating a Fahim Gabir, Abdallah Parham or Kian Majid," he finally answered, equally puzzled.

"I contacted immigration and they said they had concerns. I was told they passed the cases to ASIO to crosscheck the backgrounds of these three university students. I'm sitting here looking at the ASIO report on my computer screen at this very moment." Tiana's eyes scanned the disturbing report on her screen. "It says they were a potential threat to Australian security and outlays a plan of action, and yet you're telling me you know nothing of this?"

Mr. Teague sounded doubtful. "How is it possible you have a copy of a classified intelligence report? And furthermore, information of that calibre would be encrypted."

"Yeah well, a twenty-year-old university student

just cracked it. You might want to work on that in the future." Tiana smiled across at Rylie in amusement.

Rylie shrugged and sank further into his chair, resting his head against the back and closing his eyes. Apparently it was time for a catnap.

"As for the report," she continued, smiling in amusement at his nonplussed attitude, "it's my guess you have a leak in your department. Whoever it is, they've deliberately let these people into the country, and then covered their tracks by deleting the files from your system.

"I only have a copy of them because they were downloaded by Hayden Brooker, presumably from the hacker's computer who had siphoned off the information for your department leak. That hacker is dead by the way." Her grim thoughts ground to a sudden halt. "One of your men, Mr. Joedy Kitson, was here yesterday to collect the files. Has he not discussed them with you? They show there is a possible terrorist attack in a matter of days."

There was a significant pause on the other end of the call. "Joedy requested permission to drive to Sydney on personal business. He said something about a family crisis but did not go into detail. He was killed in a car accident on his way home."

"You may want to make doubly sure he really is dead, Mr. Teague, because it's my bet he's the leak."

"You can count on it. I need a copy of those reports today. Can you e-mail them to me?"

"Sure, give me an e-mail address and I'll do it now."

Robert complied and Tiana attached the reports to an e-mail and hit send.

"They're on their way."

Robert must have opened the inbox on his computer. "Yes, they've arrived. I'll be in touch," he assured and hung up.

Tiana closed her mouth, unable to mention what she had found in the other files. She shook her head and uploaded the rest of the hard drive files to a secure internet storage facility. She then sent the head of ASIO another e-mail with its details and access information, so that he and his people could thoroughly sift through it all.

Finally she glanced over at Rylie to see that he had dozed off. His chin had dropped as his mouth relaxed in sleep and his breathing was shallow and steady. She shook her head and smiled. How could he sleep at such a time as this? He was still under the weather.

Her mind returned to the latest revelation in this case. They were finally getting to the bottom of this and she was eager to tell Bodhi about her conversation with Robert Teague.

* * *

The hair on the back of Rylie's neck raised and a sense of foreboding came over him. Concern nagged at the back of his mind, and the strange thing was, it wasn't coming from him. He felt like he was feeling God's concern. Having experienced this kind of awareness before, he stopped midstride and asked God to keep them all safe.

Tiana brushed past and cast him a curious frown. They were in the underground garage beneath her apartment.

Bodhi had driven her home the previous day to collect her toiletries and pyjamas before taking her to his place with their four witnesses. Her car had remained parked in the basement below her apartment for the last twenty-four hours. Now he had just dropped her home so that she could collect a few more personal items before heading back to his house for the night in her own vehicle. Rylie and Kade had accompanied her to avoid being cramped in Bodhi's car.

Kade came down the stairs into the garage carrying Tiana's overnight bag. "Wow, this thing is heavy! What is it with women and their need for stuff?"

Tiana was only two years older than him and seemed to think he was positively adorable. She passed him an indulgent smile. "It's just one of those things in life that go together. Riches and fame, death and taxes, and women and stuff." She fished in her purse for the keys to her white Toyota land cruiser.

Rylie shadowed her to the car. She drew her keys from her purse and fumbled with them in the lock for a moment before they slipped from her fingers. They landed on the concrete floor with a jingle and she growled impatiently under her breath.

Rylie watched her bend to retrieve them. Her mobile phone toppled from the open mouth of her purse and slid under the vehicle. He figured he should be chuckling at her string of clumsiness, but a strange heaviness pressed upon him and instead he earnestly prayed. Something was very wrong.

Tiana dropped to her knees. As she was reaching for her phone, muttering over the fact that the screen seemed to have cracked, she appeared to glimpse something that caught her interest. She glanced to her left and frowned in bewilderment.

"What is that wad of clay with wires attached? It's near the engine."

Rylie could see the moment realisation slammed into her like a freight train. Blood drained from her face.

"Guys, there's something under here, and I think it's a bomb."

20

Rylie watched police come and go through the muster room windows, which looked out into the main headquarters. Desks were crowded into the open workspace like cattle in a semitrailer, and officers bustled about with a sense of purpose and urgency.

After Tiana's discovery of the bomb beneath her car, the three of them had been quickly ushered back to the office while it was defused. Interviews had shortly followed and now Rylie was stuck here waiting, along with Lachlan, Kade and Charlotte while talk of witness protection circulated the air.

"I'm dying for a cup of coffee," Charlotte remarked and wandered to the kitchenette against the far wall.

The room was rectangular and quite large. A door opened along the wall of floor to ceiling windows, which allowed clear visibility of the main headquarters work area. The muster room sported a dark blue suede couch positioned against the wall of glass, and several comfortable armchairs in matching material at each end. They formed a cosy nook to relax and converse.

A large dark wooden dining table, probably also used for meetings, filled the centre of the room. Against the plastered wall adjacent to the inward looking windows, was a long bench into which was built cupboards, an oven and a kitchen sink. A microwave sat upon the bench beside the sink and a refrigerator at the end. A tank of drinking water sat against the wall opposite the door, as well as a low, lengthy bookshelf full of folders, manuals, books, and the occasional magazine.

A potted plant with large green fronds stood at the end of the bookshelf closer to the far wall, and next to that was a fish tank with tropical species gliding calmly through the arrangement of underwater plant life. At the far end of the room was a ping-pong table, which by the worn looks of it, received a lot of use.

Lachlan wandered off to visit the men's room while Charlotte set about making herself a cup of coffee. Kade occupied the left end of the couch and Rylie the adjacent armchair, his thoughts in a quandary.

Rylie had searched his heart for anything that might possibly be contrary to God's expectations and found several attitudes and actions that had required he apologise. However, with his life set in order before his Maker, he still could not fathom why he was embroiled in this mess.

Had he been where God had wanted him? Had he stepped out of His will? Had Rylie caused all of this? For all his rationale told him it had been Hayden's nosiness and subsequent actions that had brought the world crashing down around Rylie's ears, he could not shake the nagging doubts now plaguing his mind that somehow he had brought this upon himself and these good people. He was fighting an age-old battle between doubt and truth, and he was no longer sure which was which.

"Please, God, You know all I want is to honour You," he whispered in an earnest prayer, forgetting entirely that he had company. "Why is this happening? What have I done?" His fingers absently rubbed the blond stubble growing steadily along his jaw line.

"You haven't done anything," Kade assured compassionately.

Rylie glanced up at him in surprise, not having expected an answer. "Sorry." He sighed and wearily rubbed his face. "I forgot I wasn't alone."

Kade observed him thoughtfully. "You remind me Job right now. You know, the guy from the Bible who lost everything; his family, his possessions, the whole lot."

Rylie levelled him with a wry look. "I know who Job is."

Kade raised his hands in surrender. "I figured you

might, but you never know."

Rylie let his head fall back against the armchair and suppressed the frustration rising within him. This had better be going somewhere, because right now the last thing he wanted was superfluous conversation when what he really needed was answers. "Why do I remind you of Job?"

Kade's long legs were stretched out in front of him and his right arm ran along the back of the couch. His left was upon the armrest. His expression was pensive as he formulated what he wanted to say.

"Job had to put up with a bunch of friends who were telling him God was against him and he had lost everything because he must have done something wrong. The suffering he had to endure was so bad he wished he had never been born.

"The mind is our biggest battleground in life," he noted, "and right now that is exactly where the enemy is trying to defeat you. Satan tried to get Job to curse God and walk away from Him by tearing his life to shreds, and finally by giving him terrible boils from head to toe. You can bet it was painful and that the temptation to walk away from all he knew to be true was great. I guess that's kind of where you're at."

Kade looked at him astutely. "You've been framed and your reputation destroyed. Your friend was killed and your girlfriend nearly died. You've been shot and struck down with an infection. Your life right now stinks and it's easy to see how you would struggle with doubt."

His understanding gaze rested upon Rylie, who looked positively worn out. "But there's something you've got to remember about Job and about God. It wasn't God punishing him or trying to destroy him, and in that very first chapter of the book of Job it states that he was blameless, upright, he feared God and shunned evil."

Kade leaned forward and rested his elbows on his knees. "Rylie, that's you. God isn't out to get you, and none of this is your fault. The enemy of your soul wants you destroyed because God has big plans to use you to bring Him honour. That is the last thing Satan wants. He wants to drag down to hell everyone God loves. That is what the terrorist threat is really about, as well as the shooter and the bomb."

Kade looked into Rylie's exhausted eyes. "The shooter and the terrorists are just pawns in a greater scheme to strike at the heart of God, by taking out as many people as Satan can. God is using you, and us, to stop that happening and to share His truth and love with those around us.

"Truth and love overcome evil every time. We've already got the victory in our hands. Jesus won it for us when He removed every barrier between us and

God and defeated death by coming alive again. We've got the victory, Rylie. Don't believe those doubts and lies for one second."

Reassurance and encouragement banished the murky depths of doubt that had been swirling inside Rylie's heart. The corners of his mouth finally lifted in a cagey smile.

He had watched the way Kade interacted with Charlotte, and the way the older man's gaze softened and followed her whenever she was in a room. Now having a glimpse of the strong faith he possessed, Rylie realised the answer to a prayer he had prayed a year ago.

Kade could not resist an amused, if not intrigued smile in return. "What?"

Rylie studied him knowingly for several silent seconds. "Kade Haynes, I've been praying you'd come along."

Kade frowned in bewilderment. "Huh?"

Rylie's grin was mischievous. "I've been asking God to send Charlie a husband whose faith is deep, and He's finally come through."

Kade's brows shot up in his tell-tale surprised reaction. "But I thought that you-"

Rylie snorted in amusement. "That she and I were going out?" He feigned a horrified shudder. "That'd be like dating my sister."

Kade sat back against the couch, his face registering astonishment. That slowly gave way to a roguish smile. "Well how about that."

"How about what?" Charlotte broke into their conversation. She wandered into hearing range and sat down beside Kade on the couch with a steaming mug of coffee.

"Oh nothing," Kade answered mildly, unable to disguise the happy twinkle in his eyes.

"Chicken," Rylie accused with a teasing smile aimed his way.

Charlotte glanced at them in confusion and opened her mouth to ask what was going on. Lachlan chose that moment to enter the room and loudly declare he was bored and someone had better verse him in table tennis.

"I will," Kade quickly offered, extricating himself from the intelligent scrutiny of a pair of beautiful light blue eyes.

Tiana was in Bodhi's office. They had gone over the evidence gathered at the scene and then the incident itself several more times. Bodhi was in his desk chair and Tiana was pacing the room.

She dropped into the spare chair that faced him.

"What do we do now?"

"We do what the detective senior sergeant says and take ourselves and our four witnesses to a safe house."

"I know that," Tiana snapped with some irritation. "I meant what do we do about the case? We can't just hide while we wait for ASIO to figure out what's going on. We need to catch the shooter. It's my bet he's a hit man for Joedy and I think it was probably him who planted that bomb. Do you suppose he's ex-military?"

Bodhi had already been considering that possibility and his look was grim. "It's likely. Something tells me we won't have to find this guy. He still hasn't eliminated his targets. He'll come looking for us, only this time we'll be ready."

21

"'For I am persuaded that neither death nor life, nor angels nor principalities nor powers, nor things present nor things to come, nor height nor depth, nor any other created thing, shall be able to separate us from the love of God which is in Christ Jesus our Lord.'" Rylie read the end of Romans chapter eight aloud, drinking in its comfort.

He re-read the last two verses and two phrases caught his attention. The first being, '...neither death nor life...', and the second, '... nor things present nor things to come...'

He was sitting at the table in the muster room. It was late and still having no answers, Bodhi and Tiana had decided that the police headquarters was the safest place they could all be right now. The boys were crammed into Bodhi's office on blow up mattresses and Charlotte was in Tiana's, while the squad worked around the clock.

Unable to sleep for the nagging doubts again pressing relentlessly into his consciousness, Rylie had dug up a copy of the Bible that had been squashed between some magazines on the muster room bookshelf. He poured over the text before him, allowing it to sink deep into his spirit.

Neither death nor life, nor things present nor things to come. He found that comforting. At the moment it was not death that scared him, but rather living and facing the uncertain future.

Once again his life had been altered irrevocably. He had the strangest impression that he would not be able to go back to the way things were. University seemed so trivial and empty now. He wanted the rest of his life to count for something lasting and meaningful. Although there was nothing wrong with a career as a computer technician, it had strangely lost its appeal.

His mind turned to their situation and he knew that only God could solve it. A fission of fear spiralled through him. The hit man was indeed being used as a pawn, and he would destroy Rylie and his friends in a heartbeat if he got the opportunity.

Rylie remembered that cold voice back in the bunker laced with malicious intent, and he shuddered involuntarily.

Do not fear any of those things which you are about to suffer. Be faithful until death, and I will give you the crown of life. The strange impression nudged his awareness.

Rylie frowned. *Until death? I am to die then?*

There came no reply and he presumed it was because the future was not something he needed to
know. God held him in the palm of His hand. He concluded that all he had to do was stick by Jesus' side
and be faithful. The rest was up to Him.

Australian soldiers poured into the third storey
apartment building in a poor section of Baghdad.
The room was sparsely furnished, with mats on the
floor for sitting and sleeping, a few cushions, an old
scratched table with rickety chairs of equal vintage,
and a clothesline strung from one corner of the
square room to the other.

In the corner was a small television sitting on the
floor, plugged into the only socket in the room. A
doorway led through to a tiny, rough looking kitchen
and presumably a bathroom.

A middle-aged woman rose from a chair at the
table. Her wide, fearful gaze encompassed the group
of five military men all carrying automatic weapons.
They swept through her home and she screamed.
Her hands flew to her cheeks and she backed toward
the wall, emitting another terrified cry.

"Do not move," the team leader commanded in

Arabic, keeping his eyes on her as his men methodically searched the apartment.

The youngest member of his team came through the kitchen doorway into the living room. His weapon was looped over his shoulder on a strap and in his hands was a wad of papers secure in a sealed plastic bag.

"Sir, we've found something," he said in clear English. "It was hidden in the toilet tank. Jonesy was in the drug squad back in Melbourne before the army and thought to lift the lid and take a look inside." He handed over some papers in a sealed bag.

The commander's eyes lit with a gleam of success. He unsealed the bag and withdrew the documents. He glanced up at the terrified woman quivering against the far wall, tears streaking down her face.

"I am sorry to frighten you," he apologised in her language, softening his tone. "We suspect your husband Ahmed has been working with Al Qaida. Can you tell us where he is?"

She looked positively shocked and shook her head. "He said he was asked by his boss to take a delivery to a customer in Karbala."

"When did he leave?"

Her worried eyes clouded with tears and droplets spilled over dark lashes onto her already damp cheeks. "Yesterday."

"That's a two to three hour return trip," the most seasoned member of his team commented from the edge of the room. He had returned from searching the kitchen. He too had learned the native language. "He should have been back the day he left."

Commander Watkins scowled as he spread the documents on the table and briefly scanned their contents. He focused on the world map where each of the major cities in the western world was circled. However, his eyes traced the trail highlighted from Baghdad to Jordan and then on to Jerusalem.

"He's not headed for Karbala. Baz, come take a look at this." He waved his comrade over and pointed to the Arabic words scrawled next to Jeru-salem. When translated, they said simply 'Day of vengeance'. "He's headed for Ar Rutbah and then the Jordan border. Our man is on the move. Let's brief Intelligence and get those borders closed down."

"Are you sure she's not in on it?"

Robert Teague was conferring with General Kincaid who was on the ground in Baghdad. The man was working with the local authorities to help establish their new democratic government. In this case, they had acted on Australian intelligence information and searched the apartment of Ahmed Rahim. It had paid off.

"No. She knew he did not favour American and Australian military presence in Iraq, but she had no clue he was involved with Al Qaida.

"Robert, I don't need to tell you that this is huge. The documents we found outline a plan for a coordinated terrorist attack worldwide. These kids you told me about have no idea what they've stumbled upon. They may very well have saved millions of lives," General Kincaid commented.

"Do you know how many cells are involved and where they are planted?"

"That's the thing. The documents contain names and contact details. This is the biggest slip up we've ever encountered in the terrorist organisation. Israeli, British and U.S authorities are already taking people into custody as we speak. Have your people located the two cells in Australia?"

A furrow permanently creased Robert's brow. "Special operation groups in Melbourne have arrested six people already. The cell in Sydney is comprised of another six, three of whom we have in custody. The other three are exchange students at Sydney University. We're only minutes away from detaining them.

"Has the media gotten wind of this yet? If they do

it could be catastrophic. It would send the rest underground or pre-empt an early strike."

"No. So far all communications between nations and government agencies have been encrypted."

Robert restrained a smile when he thought of Tiana and her student sidekick. "We're going to have to change our codes."

"Have they been compromised?"

"Yes, but so far only by the good guys. Have you found Ahmed?"

"Not yet."

Robert frowned with dissatisfaction. "Hmm." Criminals were also human, which meant that they almost always made a mistake while covering their tracks. It was only a matter of time before Ahmed made another blunder. "Keep me updated."

"I will."

The satellite line disconnected. As it did, the door to Robert's office opened and a trusted senior officer, Mark Waycott, stepped in. He closed the door but remained standing. His expression was grave, causing Robert a moment of anxiety.

"You've found them?"

Mark's eyes held no glimmer of triumph. "Yes sir."

"And?"

"They're dead, both with gunshot wounds straight through the heart," Mark replied grimly.

"The same shooter who tried to take out Rylie Hunter, Kade Haynes and Charlotte Mickleson?" Robert guessed.

Mark shook his head. "We don't think so, sir. These were professional hits made with sniper bullets from at least one-hundred yards away. We're looking into it, but so far forensics doesn't believe it was the same shooter."

Robert sighed with frustration. "So there's another killer out there."

It was a statement, nevertheless Mark answered. "It seems that way."

Robert entertained a chilling deduction. "You don't suppose it was Joedy, do you?"

Again Mark shook his head. "No. He's alive, that's for sure. His bank account emptied out this morning and we were able to trace the transfer to a foreign account in Dubai. Airport security footage picked him up three days ago boarding an international flight. He's not even in the country."

"He's headed for Dubai?"

"We think so."

"Do we have a man there on his trail?"

"Yes sir."

"Excellent. Inform me when we have him."

"Yes sir." Mark nodded and left as quietly as he had come.

Meanwhile Robert rose from his chair and stood at his window. It was dark outside, however it did not matter that he could not see the usual scenery, for his mind was elsewhere.

They were moving in for the capture, but what concerned him were the three men out there moving in for the kill.

22

Saturday: six days until the day of vengeance.

"We've got a lead on the shooter." Bodhi poked his head in the door of Tiana's office. "A street camera in central Sydney picked up his number plate after his attempt to kill Charlotte and Kade."

Tiana glanced up from the files Robert Teague had kindly forwarded. They included autopsy, ballistics and forensic reports of the two university students who were part of the terrorist cell in Sydney. Fahim was still at large. Although, it appeared there was someone else out there who wanted him dead as well.

"That was too easy. They could be fake tags," she warned him lest he get his hopes up.

"They were. Nevertheless, police picked up the fake tags ten minutes ago when the guy parked outside a railway station in the suburbs and caught a train. They're tailing him even as we speak. The description they gave matches the photograph Lachlan provided us."

It was now Saturday, two days after the bomb scare with Tiana's car. The four witnesses had been moved to a quiet motel under police guard, where they all awaited a resolution to the situation. Tiana hoped this was it. She followed her partner as he turned and jogged to the exit.

"You owe me rent at hotel rates," Charlotte informed Rylie in a businesslike tone.

Rylie exhaled in defeat and handed over a couple of hundred dollar bills. "This is ridiculous. It's not like I wanted to stay there anyway."

Kade looked sympathetic. Charlotte owned all of the decent rent paying properties on the Monopoly board and she was squeezing every last dollar out of them.

"Are they really coming?" she changed the subject abruptly. A hint of anxiety edged her tone.

Rylie watched Kade roll the dice and move six squares. "Who?"

He landed right on Mayfair, which was loaded with a hotel and houses. Rylie winced for his friend. That move was going to cost. Kade counted his limited cash, passed it to her and then handed over the last of his mortgaged properties. Charlotte did not notice that she had cleaned him out.

Kade watched her as she chewed her lower lip and fretted over the upcoming visit, unable to stop the smile that played about his lips. It was obvious he found her adorable.

Rylie on the other hand, was losing his tolerance for her ruthless business acumen and his brows drew together in an irritated frown.

"My mum and dad."

"Yes. Bodhi said they're arriving tonight on a Qantas flight." He remained fixated on her excessive winning streak. She wasn't even concentrating properly and she had still managed to wipe them out.

"How do you suppose they'll react?" she wondered aloud.

Rylie sighed in exasperation and leaned back his chair. They were sitting around the circular dining table in the motel room with the board game spread between them. Lachlan was reclining on one of the single beds by the window, playing games on Rylie's laptop. The officer on guard duty was making a cup of tea in the small alcove near the door, opposite the bathroom.

"Bodhi told them everything that's happened. They know about the amnesia, Chaz," Kade assured her.

"I know." A worried crease appeared between her brows. "I still can't help thinking that-"

"Give your Type A personality a rest, Chaz," Lachlan chipped in from across the room. "It will be what it is. They love you, they're coming, you can't remember them from Adam, but hey, who cares? You're alive, right?" He shrugged nonchalantly.

"It's easy for you to say." Kade stood and stretched. "I'm going to the dining room for some food. Anyone else hungry?"

Lachlan glanced up from the laptop screen. "Why not just order in?"

Kade answered with a hint of exasperation. "Because I'm not used to being couped up all day between four walls. I need some fresh air."

"I'll come," Charlotte offered. "Is it alright if we go to the dining room for a while, Constable?"

Constable Shelly Hobson dunked her teabag one more time and answered while she added milk. "That's fine with me. I'll tag along. You boys behave yourselves." The tall, uniformed woman in her late thirties gave Rylie and Lachlan a teasing glance.

Rylie got up sluggishly from the table and crossed to the bed where he flopped in a heap. The infection seemed to be beaten, however he still looked a little drained. He stared wearily at the ceiling. "You won't get any trouble out of me."

The officer smiled, took her teacup and followed Kade and Charlotte out the door, locking it behind her. The dining room was a large rectangular space with a bar at the far end. Huge windows ran along one entire wall looking out onto a well-manicured, secluded garden.

It was early in the evening and not many patrons had arrived yet for dinner. Small square tables draped in white linen, with stainless steel cutlery and wine glasses arranged primly on top, dotted the room in an aesthetically pleasing display. It was not fancy, but it was attractive.

Constable Hobson took a seat at a small two-person table in the far corner, where she had a clear view out the window toward the car park, as well as the entrance to the room. She picked up a menu and began perusing her options.

"Aren't you eating with us?" Kade asked in surprise as he politely held Charlotte's chair for her.

The observant woman smiled and her eyes gleamed with secret knowledge. "No, I'm fine here. You two enjoy a quiet meal together."

Kade accurately read her matchmaking intentions and smiled in amusement. At that moment he liked her very much. He seated himself across from Charlotte and drank in every detail of her face as she concentrated on her choices for dinner.

His gaze slid to her hands. They were slender but strong. He could not imagine her using them to arrest someone or defend herself in a brawl situation, and yet like everything else about her that he was discovering, he did not doubt that she could accomplish it.

Rylie had been able to fill in a little more of her past over the last few days, and it only confirmed what Kade had already suspected. She was strong willed, adventurous and fiercely independent.

A smile of pure mischief toyed with his lips. Those traits did not bother him in the least. In fact, he liked them. Life with her would never be dull.

It had taken him only four days to fall in love with her and all of two more to decide that this was the woman he was going to marry. He supposed it was fast, but then again he had been praying for a wife just like her for five years. He knew a God-given answer when it fell in his lap, and there was no way he was going to let her get away.

She suppressed a smile while her eyes were still on the menu. "What are you staring at?"

"The woman I'm going to marry," he stated boldly, that mischievous twinkle glittering in the gaze that regarded her in unabashed enjoyment.

Her wide eyes snapped up to meet his and her jaw dropped ever so slightly. "Is that so?"

"Yep."

Charlotte's expression said that she thought he had lost his good sense. Apparently she was not one to rush into things. Her gaze narrowed in amused defiance. "That's what you think."

Kade did not seem put off in the least. In fact, his face lit with the delight of a challenge.

"Can you see him?" Bodhi transmitted over a hand held radio.

Beside him Tiana and two uniformed police officers waited patiently for the target to arrive.

"Yes. He's moving toward the doors. He's getting off," the officer tailing the suspect replied over the radio.

He had followed the shooter from the suburban stop, changing over at Central Station. Now they were pulling into the underground station adjoined to the airport.

"Roger that. We're moving in." Bodhi's eyes scanned the platform where people were simultaneously boarding and disembarking.

Tiana spotted a man roughly five foot seven inches in height, wearing trendy faded jeans and a black hooded windcheater. His dark hair was shaved to within half a centimetre of his skull and his hardened green eyes were intent upon the direction in which he strode.

"There he is!" She pointed to the suspect who was heading toward the tunnel connecting the station to the airport.

The team of four started after him. Two officers moved to the right and Bodhi and Tiana the left as they entered the underground walkway. All seemed silently pleased. Two more officers were waiting at the other end.

The thick crowd coming and going made it difficult to keep track of the man, however Bodhi's height gave him an advantage. His eyes never left the target, just as a lion's would remain glued to its prey.

The shooter's head turned, his seemingly casual gaze sweeping the crowd behind him. A flash of blue closing in must have caught his attention, for he suddenly bolted.

"He's seen us."

Bodhi's radio added to the din of the busy tunnel. He keyed the microphone to reply as he broke into a run. "Be ready at the other end." Every possible exit was covered, thanks to the quick thinking of the Sydney police department.

Bodhi dodged a woman with a large suitcase on wheels and then leapt over a busker's open guitar case that was dotted inside with coins. "We're herding him to you."

He pushed between two businessmen striding

toward the airport with briefcases in hand, and then ground to a halt. Ahead he could see the end of the tunnel, and even the two uniformed officers that had been chasing the suspect with him. However there was no felon.

Bodhi growled under his breath and scanned the sea of faces around him. "Pull back!" he ordered over his radio. "He's blended into the crowd."

Tiana, who was several paces behind her partner, carefully scrutinised the crowd. She was too short to see over their heads, yet in one way her lack of height was a bonus. To have blended in, the suspect would have ducked and possibly doubled back with the flow of traffic.

She dropped her gaze from faces to feet, searching for a pair of faded denim jeans with fashionable holes in the thighs and knees. She pushed through the press of bodies and stopped when a black windcheater entered her field of vision. It had been cast aside near the far wall and was being trampled underfoot.

Tiana changed directions and headed back toward the station. She reached the entrance to the walkway and strode into the clearing, her eyes darting every which way. Finally she surveyed a newsstand nearby on her right and caught a glimpse of familiar denim pants heading into a restroom just beyond it.

She glanced behind to see where Bodhi was. She started with fright to find him directly behind her. Amusement lurked in the umber depths of his eyes.

"You nearly scared me half to death! I think he went in there." She pointed to the men's room ahead on their right, her pretty face wearing a scowl.

Bodhi only grinned. "Stay here and monitor everyone who goes past." He drew his handgun.

Tiana's glower deepened. She preferred to go in with him. Nevertheless she obeyed, understanding his logic. If the shooter was not in the toilets, then more pairs of eyes needed to be on the railway platform should he choose to seek escape by stepping onto the next train.

Bodhi warily opened the bathroom door and stepped inside. It swung shut behind him.

Bodhi began to methodically check each cubicle. His heart hammered against his chest. Finding the last one as empty as the rest, his frustration mounted. The only occupant of the room was a man in his early twenties wearing jeans and standing at the urinal. His alarmed brown eyes noted the detective's gun.

"It's okay," Bodhi assured him. "Police business.

Carry on." He mentally cringed.

That was smooth!

He strode to the door and reached for the handle. On the other side he heard a deep male voice.

"Drop the gun, sweetheart, or you're history."

Tiana!

What should he do? He could use his radio, only that would cause a standoff when the other officers swarmed to the scene.

"That's right," the voice on the other side of the door said smoothly. "Now, you're going to help me get out of here or I'll-"

Bodhi thrust open the toilet door and felt it collide heavily with someone on the other side. While he had the element of surprise, he quickly slipped out, his handgun swinging down toward the two people sprawled on the cement floor.

Tiana was clutching her cheek and a man in trendy faded denim rolled and came up on one knee, pistol in hand. Bodhi's gaze locked with a pair of cold green eyes. The barrel of each gun took aim. Bodhi pulled the trigger first.

His bullet caught the gunman in the shoulder and he jerked with the impact. The resulting shot from the shooter's weapon ploughed into the tile wall several inches from Bodhi's ear.

Heads all over the platform swivelled and terrified

screams bounced off the walls and high ceiling. Panicked travellers ducked for cover.

Tiana made a grab for the suspect's pistol that was still gripped tightly in his right hand. Malevolent green eyes went cagily from the woman wresting his gun away, to the tall detective aiming a revolver at his head. Struggling would only get him killed. He let her take it.

Tiana quickly got to her feet and collected her own weapon, which she had laid on the ground in preference to getting shot.

"Don't you so much as twitch," Bodhi warned the man.

He noted the army of blue charging toward them. Backup had arrived.

23

"Who was he?" Robert Teague asked that night.

He and his men were obviously working late, doing their best to track down Joedy and missing cell member, Fahim Gabir.

"Abraham Morgan," Bodhi answered from his desk chair, phone receiver to his ear. "He had no criminal record, but we were able to find information with the help of the armed forces. He wouldn't talk but I noticed he had a special ops tattoo on his right upper arm."

Bodhi twirled his empty coffee mug idly on the desktop and blinked when it blurred slightly around the edges. He was exhausted. Hopefully now that they had caught the shooter, he would be able to get some sleep.

"He's military?" Robert clarified.

"Ex-military. Seems he was dishonourably discharged for using excessive force to extract information from Taleban sympathisers in Afghanistan." Bodhi withheld the truly gruesome details he had uncovered.

Abe Morgan was a nasty piece of work. Rylie was lucky to still be in one piece after his first encounter with the man.

"Are you positive he is Rylie Hunter's kidnapper and also the shooter from the botanic gardens?"

"One-hundred percent. Rylie made a positive ID over an hour ago, as did Kade Haynes and Charlotte Mickleson. This is our man. The question is, who does he work for?"

"We may be able to help with that," Robert offered.

Bodhi was curious. "How?"

"It's a hunch at this stage, but I would stake my life on it," Robert hedged. "Does Abe Morgan have a cell phone?"

"Yes. I was going to have Tiana trace the calls he made tomorrow."

"I'm going to give you a number. Write it down," Robert instructed.

Bodhi inwardly sighed and recorded the digits quoted to him. "Whose cell phone is it?" he asked with mild interest.

"A burn phone we've traced to Joedy Kitson's current location. See if you can match it. We've traced his whereabouts to Dubai after he faked his own death."

"Alright," Bodhi agreed, this time with an audible

sigh. "We'll crosscheck it tonight and get back to you."

"Good. Talk to you soon." Robert disconnected the line.

Bodhi rubbed his face again and sat the phone back in its cradle. "Tiana!"

His partner appeared in the doorway of his office with an unhappy scowl. Clearly she did not appreciate being summoned with a bellow. Her right cheek was bruised and swollen from its collision with the men's room door, and her eyes were bloodshot from lack of sleep.

"Sorry to do this to you, but I need you to crosscheck the calls made from Abe's cell phone and see if this number comes up." Bodhi tore off the top sheet from his jotter pad on his desk and passed the phone number to her.

She took it and a hand went stubbornly to her hip. "It's eleven pm."

"I know."

"I'm tired and I've got a headache."

"Like I said, I'm sorry. Robert Teague requested it personally." Bodhi shrugged helplessly.

Tiana turned and grumbled under her breath all the way to her office. Bodhi could not resist a smile as he rose stiffly and followed.

"That was weird," Charlotte remarked dryly and joined Kade and Lachlan at the ping-pong table in the police station muster room.

"How did it go?" Kade referred to her meeting with her parents. They had arrived not long after the shooter had been caught. She had identified Abe Morgan and then spent the next hour talking with her folks.

"They felt like total strangers. They insisted I go home with them, although they didn't seem surprised when I said no. They're a total mystery to me."

Lachlan snorted in amusement and Kade suppressed a smile. Charlotte noticed.

"What?"

Kade hit the ping-pong ball back to Lachlan, who with a masterful downward slash sent it over the net again straight into his stomach. Kade frowned and tossed it to his friend.

"Chaz," he began and sailed the ball back to Lachlan after a rather brutal serve, "they know you, even if you don't remember them. You are the most hard-headed, independent, stubborn woman on the face of the-" Kade's observation was cut short by a fast backhand from Lachlan.

The ball hit the edge of the table on Kade's side

and bounced off, landing in the fish tank. Charlotte's eyes drilled into his broad back as he retrieved the ball.

Lachlan's right brow arched. "Mate, do you wanna die? She's shooting death rays at you."

Charlotte's gaze swung to Lachlan and he placed his bat on the table. "This would be the point in time where the trusty sidekick makes a hasty exit." He winked at Charlotte and strolled from the room.

Kade's sparkling eyes studied Charlotte's profile. She looked ready to throttle Lachlan. Then those icy blue depths swung back to him.

She crossed her arms in challenge. "You were saying?"

Kade thought she was so cute when she was mad. He supposed a wiser man would resort to discretion. However Kade had never been a big fan of tact and decided to press his luck.

"I said that you're independent and stubborn. Your parents know not to argue when you've made up your mind."

Her eyes narrowed dangerously. "And you've come to this conclusion having known me for only six days?"

Kade's easygoing grin was maddening. "Beautiful, I came to that conclusion after two."

Charlotte's jaw dropped incredulously and she

drew a deep breath, ready to give him a piece of her mind. His eyes gleamed merrily and his smile broadened. That he was enjoying her ire immensely was clearly infuriating her. Obviously realising she would get nowhere arguing the point, she simply stared at him.

He was unfazed. "You can stand there giving me daggers, or you can pick up Lachie's bat and use some of that anger to verse me in a game of table tennis."

Charlotte snatched up Lachlan's abandoned bat and stepped up to the table, too vexed to see Kade's humour and too attracted to him to walk away.

"Here you go, you can serve." He tossed her the ball.

With a mighty swipe she sailed it back. Kade reflexively turned side on as the tiny ball hurtled toward him. Instead it bounced off his upper arm, leaving a minor stinging sensation. He burst into laughter and a mischievous smile tugged at Charlotte's lips.

"Feeling better?"

"A little," she confessed with a cheeky gleam.

"Glad to be of service."

The tension inside Charlotte seemed to loosen and she laughed. He could see she was finding it hard to remain cross with him for any length of time.

24

"Bodhi, we've got him!" Tiana informed her partner enthusiastically over the phone. She was still in her office.

Bodhi turned right at Alfred Street near Circular Quay Station and pulled over, his cell phone to his ear. "Who?"

"Fahim. He made a credit card slip at a cafe in The Rocks. His cell phone is now on and I'm tracking him on my computer. He's moving along Bradfield," Tiana hurriedly explained.

"He's headed onto the harbour bridge?" Bodhi was astonished. He was less than five minutes from where they were.

"Yes. Have you dropped the guys off?"

Their presence in his car could be a hindrance. They had spent yet another night at the station and had finally been cleared to go home. Bodhi had been about to drop Kade and Lachlan at Circular Quay, intending then to take Charlotte and Rylie to the Mickleson's hotel. His plan flew out the window in that instant.

"Reroute as many local police as possible to the area. Remember, Fahim is a serious threat."

"I already have. They're shutting the bridge down as we speak. Bodhi, this is it. Catch him."

Bodhi abruptly disconnected the line and tossed the phone to Rylie, who was sitting in the front seat. He checked his side mirrors, planted his foot and swung out into the traffic.

"Whoa!" Lachlan yelped in surprise and grasped the door handle.

Bodhi activated his police light on the dashboard. He then boldly charged through busy city traffic onto Bradfield road toward Sydney Harbour Bridge.

"I want the money, Carmen!" Joedy Kitson demanded in a fit of rage. "You said if I got those last three kids in you would double the payment. They're in and have been since January."

Carmen Romari lounged casually in her penthouse apartment. It was located in a luxurious high-rise building in central Dubai. Large windows allowed brilliant light into the open plan living area. A kitchen with black marble bench tops and stainless steel appliances was in contrast to the room's furniture.

The cream lounge suite was chic and matched the

plush carpet. The room was incredibly spacious and included a dining area by the wall-length windows, overlooking a remarkable vista. Unique skyscrapers were set against a clear blue sky. The affluent city was burgeoning amidst the sea.

"Business will not pick up until demand for my company's services increase. I predict that shall happen very soon," Carmen answered calmly. "Until then you will have to be patient like me." Her brown eyes betrayed no hint of the thoughts racing through her mind.

Joedy was scandalised. "You're broke?"

"Not as such." Carmen was cool and collected, which apparently infuriated him.

She stood, her slender frame complimented by white linen trousers and a flattering blouse in striking reds and whites. Her long hair flowed down her back in dark waves.

She was beautiful, Joedy would have to be blind not to notice. She knew most men did. She was originally from Italy. Her father had been a major corporation owner who specialised in manufacturing trains, trams and cars. On the side he had dabbled with an architectural business.

He had been successful in every venture he had undertaken, amassing billions over his lifetime. Upon his death, his daughter had taken over his role and promptly frittered away his wealth in excessive living and poor investments. Now she somehow had to get her father's companies back in the black.

Carmen considered her plan and knew a moment of frustration. The last thing she needed was her dealings coming back to bite her. Joedy would need to be eliminated. An idea formed and she smiled. It was feasible.

"Can I offer you some refreshment, Mr. Kitson?"

"No!" His nervous gaze passed over the room one more time.

"Then I shall get straight down to business. I have a small amount of cash that I have kept for such a rainy day as this." Carmen started toward the master bedroom.

"How much?"

"A few hundred thousand," she replied with a smile that did not reach her cold eyes.

"That's not what you promised." Joedy's gaze narrowed. It was clear he hated to be double-crossed.

"You will get the amount we agreed upon. Consider this a deposit on the capital." Carmen slipped into her room and took a small revolver from the top draw of her bedside table. She re-emerged and wasted no time, aiming it at his chest and removing the safety.

Joedy's stunned gaze followed her. "You'll never

get away with it. People will hear the shot."

"Of course they will." A self-satisfied smile played about her lips. She tussled her hair with her free hand and deliberately tore the front of her blouse, her eyes never leaving his. "I will tell them you attacked me and I was defending myself." She shrugged, her eyes lighting in sadistic pleasure. They hardened and her finger tightened on the trigger.

Joedy swallowed hard.

Suddenly the apartment door burst open and uniformed officers burst into the room, armed and shouting warnings. Carmen began her emotional theatre performance for the Dubai police, however they were not buying it.

Her charmed life had come to an end.

25

Bodhi pulled the car to a screeching halt at the police blockade. Two sandstone towers reached toward the sky at the entrance to the enormous bridge. The grey steel structure stretched across the blue waters below in a giant arch, and flying at its pinnacle was an Australian flag.

Across the right lane of traffic, police were thoroughly looking over drivers and passengers as they came off the bridge. Bodhi stepped from the car and strode toward the officers in charge.

In the left lane traffic had been stopped altogether. There was however, a long line of cars already on the bridge that were being searched by police as they passed by at the other end.

Lachlan craned his neck out the window to see what was going on. Kade sat quietly beside Charlotte, who looked like she wanted to get out and help with the investigation. Rylie watched the goings on with mild interest.

His parents had been in touch with him that morning, and after hearing what had transpired in their absence, assured him in no uncertain terms that they were coming home. He was relieved. He wanted some normalcy in his life again, and seeing them would be a great comfort. As his mind wandered, so did his focus.

He studied the officers in the right lane several metres away, speaking with the driver of a taxi. His gaze travelled further to the covered walkway that extended the full length of the bridge. Through the meshing he noticed quite a few pedestrians heading toward the exit, tourists who had no doubt been taking in the sights from their unique vantage point.

The distinct blue of a police uniform caught his eye. An officer was jogging onto the bridge inside the walkway, presumably to clear out the last few people on foot toward the middle of the structure.

Out of curiosity, Rylie watched people filing toward the end of the walkway roughly one-hundred metres behind where Bodhi's car was now parked. One figure in particular drew his attention.

A slim man of short stature, with black hair and dark tanned skin was amidst the tourists. He kept his face averted from the police as he passed by. He looked to be of Middle Eastern heritage and seemed vaguely familiar. Could it be Fahim? Would the police recognise him?

Rylie got out of the car and closed the door, hoping to get a better look. Whoever the man was, he had positioned himself amidst a small group of Asian tourists and it was impossible to see his face.

Kade cranked his window down. He followed Rylie's intense gaze and then studied his friend curiously. "Rylie, what is it?"

Rylie glanced at him briefly and answered as he started away. "I think I just saw Fahim."

Kade stepped out of the vehicle and Charlotte followed. Both sets of eyes followed Rylie as he strode purposefully toward the end of the bridge behind them and the entrance to the walkway. Rylie swept the crowd behind him with a glance over his shoulder. He hoped to glimpse Bodhi, but could no longer see him. Where had he gone? Should they tell someone there was a possible sighting of the suspect?

Rylie entered the covered footpath, surprised an officer was not at the entrance. The group he had been following was only a matter of metres in front of him. He scanned the faces, all engaged in excited conversation, and his gaze met with a familiar pair of brown eyes. He recognised the young man who shared some of the same classes at university. Rylie was stunned.

God, it's him. Show me what to do?

Do not fear any of those things which you are about to suffer. Be faithful until death, and I will give you the crown of life. The strange impression nudged his awareness for the second time that week.

What did it mean? Was Fahim dangerous? Somehow Rylie didn't think so, not now as he stared into eyes as frightened as a hunted deer.

"Fahim?"

The Asian tourists regarded Rylie curiously as they passed by, however Fahim stopped dead in his tracks in the centre of the pathway, rooted in place by fear. His nervous gaze travelled behind them to the police blockade roughly one-hundred metres away.

Rylie glanced that way as well, hoping someone had seen them. Charlotte was talking with two police officers and pointing their way. Lachlan was watching anxiously from beside Bodhi's car. Meanwhile Kade was striding toward them, determination written all over him.

Inexplicably, images filled Rylie's vision, taking the place of reality. He closed his eyes and then opened them, baffled to see the same thing.

A small dark skinned boy with huge frightened brown eyes crouched behind an old model Datsun, parked by the side of a street lined by dilapidated buildings. Instinctively Rylie knew he was no longer seeing an Australian setting.

The child was watching an apartment behind him billow smoke from a huge hole in the second floor.

Rubble crashed down around him, and lying nearby was a woman and two very small children, a girl and a boy. They were bloody and Rylie knew they were dead. He was horrified and in that moment felt the full measure of the surviving child's turmoil.

Suddenly the images vanished and once again he saw Fahim standing before him. Uncertainty filled him.

Was that you, God?

He had heard of God giving people such insights, and yet had never experienced it himself. No answer seemed to come, and yet deep in his spirit he felt an urgent prompting to share what he had just seen.

Fahim started forward, clearly about to bolt. Rylie held his hands up and stepped between the entrance and the frightened young man.

"Wait!" His mind dwelt on the heart-wrenching picture of that young child witnessing such a tragedy.

Fahim tried to push past but Rylie gripped his shoulders, gaining a fistful of t-shirt in each hand. He was unable to stop the tears of compassion that filled his eyes.

"It was you, wasn't it? It was you I just saw?"

Fahim saw the pain in his expression and was unable to move.

Rylie noted his confusion and hurried to explain. "I just had a vision from God where I saw a young boy hiding behind an old yellow car. The building behind him had a hole in it from a mortar shell and it was on fire. On the pavement were three bodies; a mother and two children. The little girl was wearing a red tunic and lying beside the boy was a blue cap. They were dead."

Astonishment caused Fahim's mouth to drop open ever so slightly. Then his brown eyes clouded with pain. "Who told you that?"

"It was God. I saw it moments ago. That little boy behind the car was you, wasn't it?" Rylie asserted more confidently.

"Yes." Fahim stared at him in wonder. "How could you know what happened?"

Rylie felt impressed to speak and prayed that as he opened his mouth, God would fill it. "The same God who showed me, wants you to know that He loves you. He gave me this vision as a sign so that you would understand He knows your past and sees your pain."

Fahim's eyes misted with unshed tears.

"Hey!" Kade's voice reached their ears, drawing the fugitive's attention.

Panic filled his gaze and he knocked Rylie's hands aside and pushed past, bent on escape. Behind them the policeman that had been clearing the walkway over the bridge was returning. He was roughly two-hundred metres away.

Rylie turned and watched Fahim power walk toward the entrance, disappointment rising within him. He had hoped Fahim might respond to the vision and to God, but apparently that was not to be.

Do not fear any of those things which you are about to suffer. Be faithful until death, and I will give you the crown of life, the strange impression came again.

Rylie frowned in puzzlement. Why did that verse keep coming to mind?

From the corner of his eye to his right, he saw Kade approaching on the outside of the covered walkway at a jog. Behind him a steady stream of cars cruised past as they were cleared by the police at the blockade to evacuate the bridge.

As Rylie's head turned in that direction to see if the police Charlotte had been talking to were coming to his aid, he caught a glimpse of a passerby holding something out the window of a silver Ford sedan.

The vehicle was only a matter of four or five metres to their right and was driving past at a crawl. At the same time Rylie's stunned mind realised the driver was holding a handgun, he also noted that it was pointed at Fahim.

Rylie's long legs broke into a sprint, and several metres clear of the covered walkway, he body slammed the university student. As they both fell, something pelted into Rylie's back with tremendous force, tearing painfully at his insides. He landed on top of Fahim on the pavement and felt a second agonising impact.

Fear chased through Rylie. Breathing produced acute discomfort and was terribly difficult. He knew he was dying.

Do not fear. Be faithful. I will give you the crown of life.

Snatches of the familiar verse whispered through his mind and brought peace as he struggled to stay conscious.

Kade watched the scene unfold and comprehended too late that Rylie had been shot, and that the shooter had planted his foot on the accelerator and was now speeding away.

"Somebody help!" he screamed at the top of his lungs, glancing over his shoulder at the police blockade.

Charlotte and two officers were running toward him. Kade covered the last few metres to where Fahim was pushing Rylie's deadweight off.

He rolled onto his back on the pavement and

stared wide-eyed at the sky. Kade dropped to his knees beside the wounded man. His eyes locked with Rylie's, which were just as shocked as Kade and Fahim's. He broke eye contact to look at the young Middle Eastern man also kneeling beside him.

"You saved my life," Fahim stated in amazement, taking in the blood quickly pooling beneath his rescuer.

Rylie held Fahim's anguished gaze and compassion filled his.

"Son ... of God ... loves you," he managed between rasping breaths.

Kade lifted Rylie's head and shoulders from the pavement and supported him with an arm as the young man began to choke. A trickle of blood seeped from the corner of his mouth and his face contorted with pain.

"Kade." Rylie struggled to speak. "Tell him ... about ... Jesus. Promise me ... you'll ... tell him?" He spluttered and coughed, looking as though he was drowning.

Tears stung the back of Kade's eyes as he looked into Rylie's desperate face. "I will."

Fahim glanced between the two and then up at the officers rushing toward them. His distraught gaze went back to the dying man in time to see him draw a rattly breath and then close his eyes and relax.

"Rylie!" Kade shook him. "Rylie!"

Kade laid his limp form down and stood, about to yell for help. The two police officers arrived at that moment, and he could see that more were running toward them from the blockade. Behind them another came from inside the walkway itself.

"Rylie!" Charlotte called as she advanced at a dead run, slightly behind the men now at her friend's side.

Kade took two large steps forward and stopped her from coming any closer with a solid arm. She crashed into him and would have pushed past had he not held her firmly around the waist.

"Rylie!" Her horrified gaze beheld the gathering pool of blood. "Is he dead?"

One of the two officer's by his side answered as he felt for a pulse. "Not yet. Somebody call an ambulance!"

The second tore Rylie's blood-soaked t-shirt open and tried to stop the profuse bleeding by applying pressure.

"Please God, don't let him die?" Charlotte clutched at Kade's arm and watched the police officers work to keep Rylie alive.

Kade felt shock begin to numb his senses. This could not really be happening.

26

"Was he there?" Bodhi asked late that night over the telephone.

"Yes. We have Ahmed Rahim in custody. Fahim was the link we needed to find him," Robert Teague replied from his Canberra office.

"What will happen to the boy now?" Bodhi wondered, thinking of how cooperative the young man had been. He had honestly wanted to help catch the man who had previously been his mentor.

When Fahim had expressed a change of heart regarding his mission, Ahmed had hired an assassin to kill him and his terrorist cell to keep the attack from becoming known. It was now plain to see that murder was no longer in the young man's heart.

Nevertheless, he had undergone training in a terrorist camp in Yemen before coming to Australia, and had been allowed entrance to the country illegally. There would be consequences to face, despite his assistance in catching the leader of the planned attacks.

"He'll be deported," Robert replied pragmatically. "Have your people there got things under wraps?"

Bodhi eyed the mountain of paperwork still on his desk. "Yes. We're just filling out reports."

"Alright. Good job in capturing the assassin," Robert congratulated.

Bodhi thought of the sparse cell in which he was currently being detained. "Thank you sir. He's enjoying police hospitality even now."

"Excellent." Robert's tone held mild amusement. "I'll be in touch. Good night, detective."

"Goodnight, sir." Bodhi hung up, rubbed weary eyes and went back to work.

"Police have cleared Rylie Hunter of all charges," the anchorman explained on the late night news, "when they found he had been deliberately framed. Investigation uncovered sensitive information the university student had accidentally come into possession of, that has led police to discover a worldwide coordinated terrorist attack.

"The attack was planned to take place simultaneously in every capitol city in the western world, and is believed to have been financed by Italian businesswoman, Carmen Romari. Police say she intended to profit from the attacks by offering competitive prices during structural rebuilding.

"Ms. Romari is currently in police custody in Dubai, as is Joedy Kitson, an Australian ASIO officer who is believed to have illegally arranged entry to Australia for terrorist members upon payment from Ms. Romari.

"In a strange twist of events, the leader of the planned attacks hired an assassin to kill three members of the Sydney based terrorist cell when its leader, Fahim Gabir, defected. The Sydney Harbour bridge was closed down today as a precautionary measure in case of attack.

"The assassin, whose name is yet to be released, attempted a hit on Mr. Gabir at the bridge, which was foiled when Rylie Hunter saved the young man's life by stepping in front of a bullet. Mr. Hunter was shot repeatedly and is in critical condition in hospital. He is being hailed a hero for his efforts and-"

Charlotte hit the power button on the remote by Rylie's bed. She'd had all she could take of the news. She was glad Rylie's name had been cleared, however he might not live to enjoy that fact. His life hung precariously in the balance.

The first bullet had barely missed his spinal cord and had punctured a lung. The second had damaged several vital organs. The doctors had managed to do repairs and had replaced the blood he had lost with transfusions. He was stable for now. Whether he would stay that way was anyone's guess.

Charlotte listened to the steady beep of the heart monitor and was reassured to see Rylie's chest gently rising and falling in a constant rhythm. It was a miracle he had survived. If it had not been for the intervention of an off duty paramedic from one of the cars passing by, he might not have lasted until the ambulance arrived.

She breathed another prayer of thanks and leaned back in the chair beside his bed. She rested her head against the chair back and sighed wearily. Her parents had visited and stayed for quite a while. As it drew closer to midnight, they had returned to their hotel room. Charlotte remained.

Light footfalls drew her attention to the doorway where Kade appeared. He had showered and changed his bloodied clothing. He now wore a comfortable pair of jeans and a yellow windcheater. His hair sprung out from his scalp in tight curls and his usually warm brown eyes passed gravely from Rylie to her.

"How is he?"

"Stable for now. Did you talk with Fahim?"

He entered on almost silent feet and sat in the second chair on the opposite side of the bed, close to the window.

Kade smiled. "Yes. Chaz, did you know that before

Rylie took those bullets, he relayed a vision he'd been given concerning Fahim's childhood? Fahim told me about it. He was blown away by the accuracy of what Rylie said God had shown him."

Charlotte's expression quirked curiously. "What was it?"

"He said Rylie had described perfectly the moment an American mortar shell struck an apartment building above them during their occupation of Iraq. The blast and the debris killed Fahim's mother and two younger siblings. He watched it happen."

Charlotte's heart squeezed with compassion. "How terrible!" She pondered the revelation for several moments. "Was that what started his hatred of the western world?"

Kade nodded. "When Rylie took those bullets, it changed everything. I explained how every human being is separated from God by their sins, and that His Son Jesus came to pay the price for those sins by dying for us, just like Rylie asked me to.

"Chaz, Fahim prayed with me and turned away from his hatred. He allowed Jesus into his life." Kade shook his head in wonderment.

God's ways never ceased to amaze Charlotte. Yet part of her was saddened. Why could a former terrorist humble himself and see his need for Jesus Christ, and yet Lachlan could not? Nothing in Lachlan's heart had changed. He believed he was a good person and that was enough for God. No amount of reason or argument would persuade him.

"That's wonderful." Charlotte's smile was weary, albeit genuine. "Rylie's always had a sixth sense from God. I'm not in the least bit surprised he was used in that way."

An introspective silence fell and Charlotte studied Kade quietly. He had been wonderful today. He had supported her through their ordeal and had been a great spiritual encouragement. His faith had not wavered for one moment and she deeply respected and admired him for it.

She was attracted to him, there was no doubt about it. Somehow she knew that with time it would deepen. She smiled and laid her head against the chair, closing her eyes. God was in control and she was willing to follow wherever He led.

Unfamiliar sounds drifted into Rylie's consciousness. He ventured to open his eyelids a crack, feeling groggy and disoriented. He heard the steady beep of a heart monitor and connected his strange environment to the nagging pain in his back and side.

He had survived. His thoughts returned to the

bridge and Fahim. What had happened to him? He shifted ever so slightly and immediately regretted it. His wounds sent up violent protests and he gasped. Even that hurt. He lay very still and drew shallow breaths.

The sound of heavy breathing to his left alerted him to the fact he was not alone. He rolled his head carefully on the pillow to see who was there. Kade was slouched in the chair beside his bed with arms crossed and eyes closed.

Rylie glanced slowly to his right. Charlotte was curled up in the other chair with her legs drawn to her chest and her head resting on a pillow jammed between her and the armrest. She did not look at all comfortable. Nevertheless, she was fast asleep.

Exhaustion was pulling him under and Rylie knew he would be joining them in slumber soon. But not yet. Not until he knew what had become of Fahim.

"Guys," he said in a rasping whisper, discovering too late that talking was also painful.

Charlotte roused. She opened her eyes and immediately checked on Rylie. She looked surprised and also elated to see that he was awake. She sat up.

"Kade."

Kade blinked and stretched. He glanced across at Charlotte, whose eager gaze was fixed upon the patient between them. He saw Rylie's open eyes and grinned.

Charlotte was the first to speak. She clasped his hand on the white bed sheet. "How are you feeling?"

Rylie simply squeezed it in answer and offered a weak smile. He turned his head and met Kade's kind gaze. "Fahim?" he mouthed the word.

Kade smiled. "I spoke to him as you asked and he gave his heart to Jesus."

Joy and relief overcame Rylie in a mighty rush. Tears clouded his eyes and trickled down his cheeks onto the pillow. He smiled in relief and fought back the emotions choking him. He could not afford to cry. It hurt too much.

"Thanks Kade," he whispered and felt weariness wash over him. Of their own volition, his lids closed and sleep came in to claim him. He gave in easily, his heart now restful.

Kade was struck by Rylie's compassion and zeal for the souls of others, and wondered if he cared as much about those who had yet to come into relationship with God as Rylie did. Charlotte squeezed her friend's hand and looked across at Kade, a grateful smile lighting her face. He returned it. It looked like Rylie was going to be okay.

27

Over the next two weeks, Rylie had a host of visitors. They included Pastor Lucas Kennedy and his family, Joey and Joshua Donnelly and their eighteen-month-old girl Faith. Some friends from church and university came by, and his parents who had arrived home from their overseas trip.

Kade, Lachlan and Charlotte dropped in almost daily. Charlotte's memory had returned in patches and she now recalled her family in more detail. However, at times she would ask about certain events, unsure whether they were dream or reality.

Nevertheless, she was coping well, and if Rylie's sight could be trusted, she and Kade appeared to be growing closer all the time. Life seemed to have returned to normal for everyone except himself.

Rylie pondered the future and felt certain of only one thing; he did not want to be a computer technician. Something was tugging at his heart, and he knew it was God.

He heard voices outside his room and guessed that Bodhi and Tiana had bumped into his father after their brief visit that afternoon.

"Thank you for all you've done for our son," Ezekiel Hunter was saying.

"It was a pleasure," Bodhi assured the man.

"If Rylie is ever interested in putting his computer skills to work in crime investigation, we could sure use him."

He heard Tiana's light-hearted comment and smiled.

That'll be the day!

Ezekiel's good-natured laughter drifted through the doorway.

"I'll tell him."

"It was good to meet you, Mr. Hunter," Bodhi offered in parting.

"Same to you both."

"Goodbye," Elizabeth Hunter joined the conversation.

Ezekiel entered Rylie's room and sat beside the bed. Elizabeth came in behind him and sat on the other side. Rylie met his father's gaze and responded to his warm smile with one of his own. His mother took his hand and gave it an affectionate squeeze.

"How are you doing?"

Visiting with the two detectives had worn him out. He did tend to tire quickly.

"Fine," he answered softly and smiled to reassure

her. The truth was, he was not entirely sure that he was alright. He was still bothered by the uncertain future.

"I'm going to read for a while," Ezekiel stated amiably. "Is there anything you'd like to do in particular, Rylie?"

"He should sleep," Elizabeth announced in motherly concern.

Rylie resisted the impulse to chuckle, having learnt early on that laughing was even more painful than breathing or talking. "Can you please pass me my Bible?" he requested in a whisper.

Ezekiel's eyes sparkled with affection for his son. "Sure." He complied, taking Rylie's Bible from the small stand of draws that also acted as a bedside table, and passing it to him.

"If you all want to be antisocial, then would you mind if I watched a little television?" Elizabeth asked, not in the least offended.

They visited for hours on end each day, sometimes playing chess, talking or sitting quietly and reading. They were all just grateful to be together and to know that Rylie was going to make a full recovery.

"That's fine," Ezekiel answered for his son and himself.

They settled in comfortably, Ezekiel with a novel, Elizabeth flipping through the available channels, and

Rylie with his Bible. He flicked through the pages until a passage he had highlighted years ago caught his attention. He read with interest and then with conviction.

'The Spirit of the Lord God is upon Me, because the Lord has anointed Me to preach good tidings to the poor; he has sent Me to heal the broken-hearted, to proclaim liberty to the captives, and the opening of the prison to those who are bound; to proclaim the acceptable year of the Lord, and the day of vengeance of our God; to comfort all who mourn, to console those who mourn in Zion, to give them beauty for ashes, the oil of joy for mourning, the garment of praise for the spirit of heaviness; that they may be called trees of righteousness, the planting of the Lord, that he may be glorified.'

The passage from Isaiah sixty-one was of course referring to Jesus. Yet as a follower of Christ, it also applied to him. Rylie read it a second time and at its conclusion he had his answer. He knew what he wanted to do with his future. A broad satisfied smile claimed his lips and his gaze drifted out the window.

Epilogue

Twelve months later:

A light sea breeze stirred loose curls that had escaped the pins in Charlotte's hair. The setting sun cast a golden glow upon her. The lace of her simple, white flowing gown moved with the gentle wind.

Kade's breath caught in his throat. She was beautiful. He watched her walk down the sandy aisle between chairs that were filled with family and friends and he marvelled. She had finally said yes, and the day had come.

Rylie smiled as Charlotte passed by his seat in the front row. He looked deeply happy for his friends. He was enjoying singleness and the unparalleled opportunity it gave him to reach out to others. He was training to become a pastor, and in his free time he worked with the outcasts of Sydney in a local shelter. Beside him was Sean, a fourteen-year-old street kid.

Rylie had taken the teenager under his wing, and upon experiencing God's love and grace for himself, the boy's life had taken a dramatic turn. From conversations with Rylie, Kade saw that his friend was fulfilled and loving every moment of the second chance God had given him. He seemed determined to use it to the utmost.

Today Charlotte and Kade's lives would become forever entwined. Kade's smile broadened. A ray of golden sunlight pierced the scarlet tinted clouds on the horizon. He thought it most fitting.

Dave Mickleson placed his daughter's hand in Kade's. The couple looked into each other's eyes and smiled in anticipation and love.

The sun-kissed beach stretched before them. Just like their lives, it was touched by brilliant rays beyond the stormy clouds, and full of promise.

Dear Reader,

I hope you have enjoyed this book. I certainly had an adventure preparing for it. I visited a friend in Sydney who took me on a personal tour of various famous landmarks around Port Jackson.

After that trip, I had the seed of an idea for this sequel to *Thief In The Night*. I thought it might be fun to base this book in the places I visited. That way the reader would in essence, be getting a tour of Sydney (although some writer's licence has been used).

I can't say as there is one spiritual theme that runs through this story, as I am sure there are several. I think one that I have been pondering more and more lately, however, is that which Kade points out to Rylie in a discussion. Kade mentions that the motives behind their enemy's repeated efforts to kill them, and in the pending terrorist attacks, are underpinned by a greater plot to strike at the heart of God.

This wicked plan is at work in our world and our society even now, and it pays to have our eyes of discernment attuned to what is truly going on. So often when we hear of terrorist attacks by extremists, we tend to label people and fall into the same trap of hatred and anger. Sometimes we can go as far as prejudice toward other nationalities.

Scripture says that our fight in this world is not against flesh and blood, but against Satan and his army who are trying to drag down with them as many souls as possible. They are fighting a losing battle against an all-powerful God, Whose loving heart is reaching out to save lives from a lost eternity.

Love always overcomes evil.

Fahim's encounter with God is I think my favourite in this story. It shows God's unconditional love and forgiveness. Then in Lachlan we see a common occurrence for a lot of average people: the inability to see their sin for what it is. Therefore they fail to see their need to be saved from its devastating future consequence of eternal separation from God.

No matter your past or your beliefs, there is a very loving Creator Who loves you. He sent His Son Jesus to take the punishment for your wrong doing. This punishment was eternal separation from Him. When Jesus Christ died, He paid your debt. He rose again and now works through His Holy Spirit to draw people into personal relationship.

I am sure many readers will have already experienced this. I know I have, and I can honestly say there is nothing more satisfying than walking in close friendship with Jesus.

He loves you! Perhaps like Charlotte you may need to rediscover that love. Or maybe like Fahim, it is a new concept altogether. Or are you like Rylie and Kade who have walked side by side with Jesus for many years?

Whatever your point in that journey, reach out to those nail scarred hands, and find a Friend who will stick closer than a brother. You will never regret it.

As Charlotte did, fall into the chasm of love in the Father's heart and find arms that will carry you through life's uncertain terrain.

Love in Him,

Jo His Daughter.

www.jayhdee.weebly.com